hatchet

Other Books by Emma Leigh Reed

Making the Rules

Breaking the Rules

A Fine Line

A Time to Heal

Second Chances

Trusting Love

Mirrrored Deception

hatchet

E.L. REED

ELRpublishing

Text copyright © 2021 by E.L. Reed

Published by ELR Publishing.

ISBN-13: 978-1-944550-12-7

Cover and interior design by Kenny Holcomb
kennyholcombdesigns.com

Printed in the United States of America

To Bradyn

May you always find joy in the simple things

one

The moon created long shadows between the buildings and gave the perfect cover. I darted in and out, becoming one with the shadows. My movements were hurried as anxiety rose within me, only to be outweighed by the confidence bubbling up.

I stopped and glanced into the alley before entering at a slower pace, darting my eyes from side to side, taking everything in.

The reek of urine and body odor took my breath away, and I paused. The stench of the alley didn't deter me. Instead, it spurred me on. Pressed against the wall, I blended further into the darkness and spotted him. The perfect target. The homeless man walking to the dumpster, his movements slow as he lumbered toward it and laid down his backpack next to it. This man would be the quintessential guinea pig for my plan.

He squatted by his bag to pull out a jacket, then carefully zipped up the backpack. He flailed the coat out in front of him, opening it up. My adrenaline kicked in, and I could hardly restrain myself as I watched him slide his arm into the sleeve.

I crept closer, hugging the wall. My fingers twitched around the handle with anticipation. My heart raced and I heard the rush of blood pounding in my head like a drum. The man's movements were slow, no indication that he was worried about anything around him.

I held my breath as I took another step closer, then exhaled slowly, trying to calm my racing heart. The shadows were perfectly placed, hiding my movements. I crept out from the wall, just a step away from him.

I raised my arm and brought my hatchet down with as much force as I could. The first blow struck the back of the man's neck. It hit with a greater force than I had anticipated, the blade cutting deep. His blood spattered my face and hand. The warmth of it shocked me but triggered an adrenaline rush I didn't expect as he fell to his knees.

I brought my arm back for another swing, the enticing sensation of his blood fueling me on. The second blow took him forward, face down on the ground. Since my goal was his face, I turned him over with my foot. I had a haunting urge, to mutilate the faces that haunted my dreams. And, although he was simply a guinea pig, I needed to see how erasing a face could empty my dreams…*my nightmares*.

With my right foot on his stomach, I rained blow after blow upon his face until he was no longer recognizable.

After ten strikes—or was it eleven—I stood back and surveyed my surroundings. Blood pooled beneath the man's head. Satisfied with my accomplishment, I glanced down at myself. His splattered blood covered me from head to toe. A peace settled over me at how easy it had been to take the man's life. Easy because I didn't know him? Or easy because I was finally strong enough to fight back?

I used the man's cloths to wipe off the excessive blood from the hatchet blade and carefully stepped away to avoid the pool of blood on the ground. With one more glance, I turned and hurried from the alley, staying in the shadows and out of sight.

Entering a small door in the wall, I stood still for a moment. I allowed my eyes to adjust to the darkness, then continued down a corridor until I reached the lone room at the end of the hall. There was no electricity. Only a faint beam of moonlight streamed into the center of the room from a small window near the ceiling.

A cot at the far wall stood with only a threadbare blanket across it. No pillow. The opposite wall held a little table with a single chair. I crossed the room to the table and picked up a rag, then ran it over the hatchet, clearing it of the man's hair, skin, and blood. My fingers lovingly stroked the fine weapon. This was the power I'd been searching for. For years, I didn't know how it would make me feel. But tonight, I felt a strength within I never imagined would emerge. Satisfied, I laid the hatchet on the table.

Under a candleholder at its center was a piece of paper with a black crayon next to it. I slid the paper out, picked up the crayon, and drew a thick black line through the first item on the list. After carefully placing the paper back under the candlestick, I peeled off my dark cloak and changed into clean clothes from the closet, then stuffed the blood-soaked cloak and clothing into a garbage bag. Once I cleaned my face and neck from the blood spatter, I threw the wet cloth I used into the bag with the other blood-stained items.

Inhaling deeply and exhaling slowly, I calmed my racing heart.

One down.

A smile curled up the corners of my mouth, and I gave myself a virtual pat on the back for pulling off the first—and most difficult—kill I'd have on this journey. I cautiously opened the door and ran along the hall toward the exit leading to the street.

With a quick glance around me, I exited the place and ran, careful to stay close to the wall of the buildings, blending in with the shadows, indiscernible to the world. I loved being able to disappear into an alley and from sight.

Releasing a sigh of relief, I mingled with the homeless wandering around, then crept away unnoticed. I vanished into my little world where no one knew if I was alive or not, except to kick me when I was down. There'd be a change with that. No more would I tolerate those kicks. I wasn't taking the abuse anymore. I had found my voice, and those who'd hurt me in any way had better watch out.

two

Detective Wesley Dawson made his way between cars toward the alley. Yellow tape stretched across the entrance. He bent down, maneuvered under the tape, and entered the crime scene. Blood splatter thickened as he got closer to the body lying on the ground.

He swallowed hard as he took in the scene. He'd seen plenty of blood over the years. Although he'd never been on a tour of duty while he served in the military before hurting his knee, he'd been working for the Connecticut State Police since then. Over the years, an abundance of murders had come across his desk. He'd been a rookie detective for most of them. This was the first solo case he'd been assigned, and he knew his reputation depended on the outcome.

The victim laid on his back in a pool of blood. The face unrecognizable. Dawson took it all in, not saying a word to anyone around him. He squatted down and studied the view, before moving to another angle and repeating the position, mentally taking in all he saw. He continued to make his way around the scene in the same fashion.

"What do we know?" Dawson spoke without looking over his shoulder, knowing there was a police officer right behind him.

"Unknown male. First impressions would say he was homeless."

Dawson nodded. "Time of death?"

"Waiting on Jenson to get here."

"I want to know as soon as you do." Dawson walked to the wall along the alley and studied it. Blood splatter ran up the side of it. He turned toward the victim on the ground. "Perp must have stood here."

"How do you know that?" the young police officer—pen in hand, poised over his notebook—asked.

"From the pattern of blood. Looks like the splatter runs up and over someone's head. Whatever the weapon was, there was momentum with arm swing, bringing the blood splatter above whoever stood here."

The young rookie wrote furiously.

Dawson reached out and placed his hand over the pen, then waited until the young man's eyes met his. "What's your name?"

"Brown, sir."

Dawson nodded. "Forget the sir, Brown. Put your pen and paper away. Come stand next to me and tell me what you see."

Brown quickly put the items away and stepped up beside Dawson. He glanced over at the victim, then closed his eyes briefly and looked again. "Sharp cuts on the face making it unrecognizable."

"And what does that tell you?" Dawson kept his voice calm and quiet, yet prodded the man, demanding an answer.

"If I took a guess, I'd say the weapon wasn't a knife. The blade was too big. An ax or hatchet, possibly?"

"Are you asking me or telling me?"

Officer Brown glanced at Dawson. "Telling you, sir. There are at least ten blows to the face."

"Excellent. You don't need to make notes. Trust me, you'll see that in your memory for a long time. Allow those sights to burn in there. You'll remember something you're unaware of now at a later time. It'll help you in solving this."

"Solving it?"

Dawson clapped him on the back. "Yup. We'll be in touch, so keep looking around the scene. No notes. Soak it in."

"Yes, sir."

Dawson took in his surroundings once more before moving toward the main road. As he arrived on the sidewalk, he stopped and looked around. Diagonal to the alley entrance was a small diner with neon lights flashing Open All Night. Watching traffic, Dawson jogged across the street and stood at the door, looking back to the alley. Couldn't see much, but possibly someone saw people enter the alley.

He pulled open the door and entered the diner. As he made his way to the counter, he glanced around. Sliding onto a stool, he sat half-facing the room.

"Can I help you?" A soft voice behind him broke his concentration.

"Coffee, please." He turned toward the young waitress. She was a petite thing with mousy brown hair pulled back in a ponytail. He gave her a half-smile before he realized she never looked at him. She kept her eyes on the mug as she filled it.

"Anything else?"

He flashed his badge at her. "Were you working last night?"

She nodded, glancing up to meet his gaze briefly before averting her eyes again.

"Did you hear any commotion last night or see anyone going in and out of the alley across the street?"

She looked out the window at the alley and shook

her head. "I don't pay attention much to stuff outside. Just tend to my customers." She waited a brief second before walking off to return the pot to its spot in the coffee machine.

Dawson sipped from his mug as he surveyed the place. It appeared she was the only waitress working at the moment, and the kitchen wouldn't have had a clear view of the alley. He sighed as he finished his coffee and threw down a couple of dollars, then set his cup on top of the money, along with his business card.

"If you hear of anything or remember something you might have seen, please call me," he called out as he turned to leave. He caught a glimpse of the slightest nod from the waitress before he exited.

Dawson had no sooner gotten back to his car, when his cell phone vibrated. He pulled it out and saw a message from Officer Brown stating that the coroner wanted to see him. He wished there was a lead, but knew it was unlikely this soon into the case and only hoped, at least, they got a name for the victim.

three

Dawson walked into the coroner's office. The cold sterility of the place matched his mood. Being a perfectionist wasn't easy in this job. He loved the thrill of justice when it was served, but getting there was often heartbreaking and stressful. He'd failed at being a Marine, getting injured and *honorably* discharged, but it didn't feel honorable to him when he saw no direction in his life, no stability; the thing he needed the most when he'd joined the service.

Finding this killer would serve two purposes; one, to bring him accomplishment like never before in this job and two, a sense of belonging. He knew full well he was good at his job, but sometimes it just never seemed to be enough for him.

He continued into the autopsy room to see his victim laid out on the table. The autopsy was in progress, so he stood off to the side to keep from disturbing Jenson while she recorded notes as she went along.

She paused when she saw him and motioned him over. "Glad you could join me." She flashed a smile at him.

He nodded, then stared at the victim. "Anything yet?"

Jenson shook her head. "Nothing other than time of death was close to midnight. John Doe, as of right now."

"Can you get dental records?"

"He was missing most of his teeth, but I'll try to match what he has. It's a long shot. My guess is he'd been on the streets a long time, judging by the grime on him under the bloody mess."

"Murder weapon?"

Jenson moved across the room to the computer. "From the slices that were in him, I'd say we're looking at a blade of some sort. Best guess would be an ax-type tool, possibly a hatchet, based on the size of the marks, but they overlap, so it's hard to get an accurate measurement of the size of the weapon."

"An ax is a good size. Certainly would be a good-size perp we're looking for then."

Jenson nodded. "A hatchet would be easier to handle, but until you find a weapon and I can match it, there's no definite answer there."

"At least, it's something to go on. Thanks." Dawson stopped at the door. "Let me know when you have anything else."

"Will do." Jenson dismissed him.

Dawson paused for a moment watching her, wondering how she could stand to be here day after day with the dead. He sighed and pushed through the door, aching to fill his lungs with some fresh air. Exiting the building, he stood on the sidewalk and drew in a deep breath.

He loved being a detective and bringing justice to those who had no one to fight for them, but at times, it was hard to keep the emotions out of it when dealing with the homeless. He hid this fact well from others. As far as anyone knew, he was emotionless about his job, working diligently to get answers, but never becoming emotionally involved. No one knew it shook him to the core to witness the lack of loved ones in a victim's life. He prayed he could find someone who knew this man and cared enough for him to give him a proper burial.

He pulled out his cell phone and put a call in to Officer Brown. He relayed the information regarding an ax or a hatchet and asked the officer to canvas the area looking for possible dump sites for the murder weapon. The rookie was eager to help and jumped at the chance to work with him.

Dawson turned back to return to the diner. He wondered whether regular customers might know the homeless man. If only he had a picture of him before his face had been destroyed.

The diner was buzzing. It was full, except for a couple of lone stools at the end of the counter. He sat down and looked around. The same waitress was there. He watched her casually as she took orders. She talked very little with the customers, and, in fact, the customers made repeated snide comments to her as she moved around the diner, teasing her for her lack of friendliness. Dawson kept an eye on her. No emotion crossed her face, and she just continued to work with no reaction.

When she finally got to him, he ordered coffee and a roast beef sandwich. She glanced at him and quickly averted her eyes again. Always fascinated by people-watching, Dawson sat comfortably against the back of his stool and just took it all in.

"You workin' that murder across the street?" an older gentleman called out.

Dawson turned in his seat and nodded. "Were you here last night?"

The man got up and walked over to Dawson. "No, sir, but Eugene's not been in today, and I'm wondering who it was that got knocked off."

"Eugene?"

"I'd say a friend of mine, but not sure you could say

we're friends. He always met me here in the mornin', and I bought him a hot breakfast to help him get through the day. I haven't seen him."

Dawson gestured to the stool next to him. "Have a seat." He waited until the man was seated. "Eugene was homeless?"

"Yeah, lived in the alley across the way."

Dawson closed his eyes. A name, at least. "I'm sorry. Our victim is unidentified as of right now. Do you have a recent picture of Eugene? Or does he have any family?"

The man shook his head. "No pictures and he talked of a daughter, but never mentioned her name. I don't know where she is."

Dawson pulled out his card and handed it to the man. "Please, if you remember anything else, call me." He turned to his sandwich just as the waitress set it in front of him.

"Anything else?" she mumbled.

"What's your name?" Dawson reached out a hand to stop her from walking away.

"Beth."

"Hi, Beth. Do you work every shift?" He popped a chip into his mouth, waiting.

"Pretty much. One other waitress is supposed to be working, but she's been out sick the past couple of days, so I've been working doubles. Charlie is the only one here late at night. Not much business then." She glanced around. "I'm really busy…"

Dawson nodded and watched her walk off. He dug into his sandwich and listened to the chatter behind him as people speculated about what had happened in the alley. There was no mention of anything useful, and as soon as Dawson finished eating, he stood to pay his bill.

"Beth, is the owner around?"

She nodded. "He's one of the cooks. Hang on."

She disappeared into the kitchen and returned within moments, behind a short, stout man.

"Can I help you?" The man held out his hand. "I'm Charlie, owner of this fine establishment."

Dawson gave the man's hand a firm shake. "I just wondered if I could get the name of your other waitress. How long has she been out?"

"Amy. Amy Patterson. She's been off for a few days now. Has the flu, or so she told me." Charlie grunted. "I wonder if she's not looking for another job. This one's not easy to work with." He nodded toward Beth.

"Why's that?"

"Just don't like other people. Customers prefer Amy, which she likes the tips from, but hates the extra work. When Beth's here alone, customers don't have a choice and deal with her crappy attitude." Charlie lowered his voice. "She's always been an odd one, but she's family, so I keep her on."

Dawson glanced over to Beth, who was shooting daggers at Charlie. "Thanks for your help."

Dawson walked out of the diner and sighed. Nothing much, other than an odd family dynamic. He crossed the street to the alley. It was still taped off, but empty, except for a few police officers still searching the area.

Recognizing Officer Brown, Dawson approached him. "Did you talk to any of the other homeless out here?"

"They've been few and far between. Ones I have seen, refuse to talk to me." Brown shrugged. "They won't say much to cops."

"They're protecting one of their own. Ask around for Eugene. I think that's our vic's name, but I want to be sure."

Officer Brown nodded. "No weapon, sir."

"Not surprised. Our best lead is finding out who knew Eugene. Maybe one of his friends out here saw something." Dawson turned back toward the main street. "Brown, be compassionate with them. If it was Eugene, then they've lost him and they'll need to grieve. Offer them a place to warm up at the station while we talk to them, and hot coffee…Maybe they'll talk more if they can warm up a bit."

"Yes, sir."

"Lose the sir, Brown."

It wasn't freezing outside yet, but fall weather had certainly brought cooler nights. Dawson knew how quickly some of the homeless would jump at the chance for a hot beverage and a place to warm up for a little while. He'd wandered these streets himself at night searching for his sister when she'd run away from home. Those nights had been a real eye-opener for him, and he'd gained a new respect for the people out here who seemed to have no other alternative than to live on the streets.

Sara had continued to elude him, and as frustrating as it was to search the alleys for her night after night, he kept doing it anyway.

He shook off the painful memories, then pulled out his cell phone and punched in a familiar number with determination. Listening to the rings, he knew she wouldn't answer. After the fifth ring, he ended the call and pocketed the phone. Every time he tried the number, his heart ached when he had to hang up without receiving an answer.

He put his thoughts back on his current situation and couldn't shake the sense of urgency that surrounded this case. Still, he couldn't put his finger on his reason for feeling that way.

four

The moon shined brightly, and the night was lighter than I'd hoped. It was harder to keep in the shadows. I tried to contain my excitement, but the thrill of killing the homeless man kept running through my mind. The more I thought about it, the more my blood flowed, building an anticipation for my next victim.

This time, I was ready to start fully on my list. The test victim had gone so well. Since that night, I yearned for the faces of my adversaries to stop visiting me every time I closed my eyes.

My adrenaline kicked up a notch as I started walking in the shadows of the alley. This was going to be perfect. I'd watched my next victim now for what seemed like hours, and yet, in reality, it had only been a short time. She was so full of herself and needed to be taken down a notch.

I was tired of being the brunt of the jokes and being picked on because I didn't fit a mold. I was going to make something of myself and people would remember me. No more would I sit in silence and take the abuse I'd suffered all these years.

Flashes of memories from years ago started reeling through my mind: My father hitting me when I couldn't do anything right, or visiting me at night to tell me he was making amends for treating me badly during the day. I'd have to endure his "apology" night after night.

Where was Mother in all this? She'd sit there just watching during the day and turn her head in ignorance at night. Where was my protection from this evil? A child is supposed to be loved and protected, not abused in every way day after day. Where was my happy childhood?

I snapped back to the present and refocused again on the woman. She stopped outside the alley, talking on her phone.

Bringing out my inner child, I cried just loud enough to be heard in my voice of years ago, "*Help.*"

She turned toward the sound, ended her call, and took two steps into the alley. "Is someone there?"

"Help me," I called again. My lips curled into a smile that would have made Satan himself proud.

"Where are you?" she called.

"Just down the alley. I've fallen. Help me." I almost laughed out loud, she looked so concerned. I played this part so well, my inner child constantly crying for help, and no one ever listening in years past. It was almost touching how someone finally wanted to check on a hurting child…almost.

She took a hesitant step toward me, and then another. My hand clenched the hatchet, itching to make that first strike. I forced myself against the wall of a building, deeper into the shadows of the alley. I had to be patient.

"Please hurry. It hurts," I cried out again.

Her steps quickened as she moved closer. She was so near I could smell the flowery, overpowering scent of her perfume. I had to take shallow breaths not to be overwhelmed by it. Leave it to her to be overbearing in every aspect.

My fingers tapped silently on the handle of the hatchet, waiting for her to take just a couple more steps.

"Where are you?" She pulled out her cell phone and shined a light from it around, searching the ground for the hurt child.

"Over here, against the wall." My voice was soft, yet I surprised myself at the innocent childlike urgency I conveyed.

She took those extra few steps and was right in front of me. She lifted the light of the cell phone, and it caught the hem of my cloak.

"What the—"

I stopped her voice short by the upswing of my hatchet. The back of it caught her chin and knocked her down.

"So, kind of you to want to help me." I stepped out of the shadows, wanting her to see my face. I needed her to know I could inflict more pain on her than she could ever imagine. Hatred boiled within me.

Shock registered in her eyes as she caught a glimpse of my face and recognized me. I brought the hatchet down. The first cut hit her right eye and cheek. A cry escaped her before she went silent.

I raised my arm again and the force with which it came down surprised me. Rage overtook me, and I brought blow upon blow to her face. Was the red I was seeing from the rage or from the blood? It didn't matter. It fueled my anger and contempt for this despicable person who'd hurt everyone around her with her high and mighty attitude.

Finally, seeing the sight before me, I stopped and just looked at her. She was unrecognizable—just like the homeless man. I'd demolished that face that she'd so carefully made up that day.

As I stared down at her, a sense of relief washed over me. I smugly gave her a small kick as I moved away. The blood rush I'd felt was slowing down, and I was able to decrease my heart rate as I took in the scene one more time.

After wiping the excess blood from the blade onto the victim, I turned and ran along the sidewalk, blending with the blackness of the night. The moon had slid behind a cloud as if to give me the go-ahead for my disappearance. A chuckle came from the shadows, spurring me to hurry. Not allowing paranoid to rule me, I whispered to myself. *Just another homeless person. Keep going.*

I came to the door in the wall and slipped inside. Once again, following the hallway, I slid into the lone room. There was no time to waste. I laid the hatchet on the table, stroking the blade gently with my gloved fingers before turning to the list and crossing off the next item.

A large *bang* caused me to jump. Turning toward the door, I instinctively gripped the hatchet in my gloved hand which trembled as I listened intently. No further sounds came, and I returned the hatchet to the table. I, then, cleaned up as before. Seconds ticked by as I crept down the hallway to the outside. Glancing from side to side to make sure the coast was clear, I slipped into the shadows, and once again, disappeared into the night.

five

Dawson tossed and turned all night. Images of his sister's face coincided with the homeless man's. As the dawn started to break, he rose. After splashing his face with water, he glanced into the mirror. Dark smudges under his eyes were evidence of his sleepless night. He cursed and turned the shower on. He needed the hot water to wash away the nightmares and the continued angst of not being able to find his sister, even after all these years.

He allowed the hot water to clear his mind as much as it was going to be cleared, then dried off and got dressed. He leaned against the kitchen counter, waiting for his coffee to brew. As soon as the coffee maker finished, he filled his favorite mug. With his eyes closed, he inhaled the rich aroma and allowed it to sink into his senses before taking that first-morning sip. As hard as he tried, he couldn't stop himself from this daily ritual. The strong caffeinated scent reminded him of his childhood, one he had thought was happy for him and his siblings.

Happy, until the day his sister thought she wanted more, and his parents forbade her to go. In the middle of the night, she'd packed her stuff and left anyway, leaving only a note for Dawson behind. He'd been just sixteen when she left, and he'd spent the past fourteen years searching for her every day. He'd spend hours after his work shift combing the streets for her. Every two or three years, he'd get a note from her stating she was fine. He knew she was still in the area, but even with all his resources in the force, he couldn't find her. It broke his heart.

His parents had become bitter, and soon afterward, his other two sisters had left for college, never to return to the family home. He was the youngest and had stayed longer than he had wanted, out of obligation to help his parents. But, eventually, he had to move out for the sake of self-preservation. He returned dutifully every couple of weeks to check on them, even though they acted as if they couldn't care less if they saw him. They blamed themselves for Sara's leaving, and as a result, had shut the rest of their children out of their lives. They rarely left the house, and when Dawson arrived, they refused to talk to him other than in one-word answers.

The painful reality was, Dawson had no real family left. His older two sisters had cut ties with him also, in an attempt to keep the past away from their present lives. Dawson accepted it. Sara had been the one he'd been closest to anyway, and he missed her daily.

Finishing the last of his coffee, he put the mug in the sink and stared out the window. There was a light frost on the ground. He hoped that the promise of a warm place would bring in some of the homeless people and prayed that one of them knew Eugene and could identify him. They had no hope of finding his family if his daughter had disowned him.

He grabbed his jacket and headed toward the local station. He lived only blocks away and decided to walk instead of driving. It would give him a chance to check the streets again. He walked slowly, scrutinizing every nook and cranny where one could hide. In his mind, he always imagined his sister staying close to where he lived. Somehow that thought comforted him as he mentally berated himself for not finding her.

As he reached the station, he glanced around once more. There were a lot of people hanging about; some homeless, a lot of officers, and the place was bustling with activity. He took the steps two at a time to reach the front door.

He had no sooner set foot in the door when he heard the captain's voice. "Detective Dawson!"

"Yes, sir."

"My office, *now!*"

Dawson hurried down the hallway to Captain Collins' office. He shut the door behind him and faced the local head honcho.

"Sit down."

Dawson complied and waited patiently.

"What have you done?"

"Sir?"

"I have a conference room full of homeless people expecting hot coffee and a place to *hang out for a while to warm up.*"

"Yes, sir. The victim was a homeless man. I have a lead on his name and thought the warmth would help loosen their memory and their tongues, so they could share some info."

"This isn't your charity work?"

"No, sir. Strictly related to this case, I assure you."

"Get to it then. The quicker you get through your questioning, the quicker they're back out on the street where they belong."

Dawson reached for the door to leave, when the captain's voice stopped him. "I get it, Dawson, I do. I'm not heartless, but try to stay objective on this. I understand we need to cooperate fully with you, but please don't shake up this place too much."

"Always, sir."

Dawson nodded and proceeded to the conference room. Officer Brown had gone above and beyond and filled it with dozens of donuts for the people to munch on with their coffee.

Dawson nodded at Brown as he walked by, then greeted each of the homeless individually, asking if they were warm enough. He spoke softly to keep each conversation directed to the person he was talking to, and not for everyone in the room to hear.

It took him an hour to get around the conference room to talk to everyone. Most of them had cleared out after the donuts were gone. One small woman sat huddled in the corner, shaking. Dawson couldn't tell if she shook from cold or fear. Although hard to be accurate guessing her age, Dawson thought her to be close to seventy.

"Can I get you a blanket, ma'am?" He knelt in front of her.

"No use for a blanket. I'll be warm in a minute." Her body shivered contradicting her words.

Dawson turned to the table behind him where some blankets had been left behind by others. He grabbed one for her and wrapped her up tight. "You take your time warming up."

"You're the young man that the other officer said wanted to talk to us."

"Yes, ma'am. The name's Detective Dawson, Wesley Dawson." He eased onto the floor beside her.

She flashed a toothless grin. "Good strong name." Dawson smiled and waited. They sat in silence for what seemed like ages before she spoke again. "It was Eugene, wasn't it?"

Dawson froze, contemplating her question. "I don't have a solid identity yet, but Eugene is a name that keeps coming up as someone who's gone missing. Would you have a picture of him?"

"No. But he carried a bag with pictures of his daughter in it."

Dawson shook his head. "There was no bag near the man we found." He paused. "Do you think it's possible that Eugene might have just moved on?"

"No. He wouldn't leave this area. His daughter is nearby." She leaned forward and reached her hand behind her. As she pulled it forward again, she held out a small canvas backpack. It was well-worn and filthy, but Dawson took it from her. He noted the dried blood splatter on it.

"It's Eugene's?" He knew, even before she nodded the answer. He opened it slowly and pulled out a few pictures. The same girl was in all of them. "Do you know her name?"

"Katie. I don't have a last name, 'cause she got married. But it used to be Henry, same as Eugene's."

"That will help us find her though." Dawson put the pictures back in the bag and set it down on the floor beside him. "Ma'am, where did you get the bag?"

"Name's Hannah. Don't be wasting that ma'am stuff on me. I don't deserve much respect these days, looking like I do." She leaned back against the wall, pulling the blanket tighter around her. Her shivers had lessened considerably. "I heard Eugene cry out. I couldn't see who did that to him, but after they left, I took his bag. I knew how important it was to him, and I didn't want the others to steal it. They're like scavengers sometimes, taking what doesn't belong to them. I wanted it to be saved from being torn apart by the others."

"I understand." Dawson patted her on the shoulder. "Wait here. I'll be right back."

He picked up the bag and left the conference room. "Brown!" he called to the young rookie who was chatting with another officer.

"Yes, sir."

"Get this bagged as evidence. Pictures of Eugene's daughter are in that bag. Her name is Katie. Maiden name was Henry. Don't know her married name, but see what you can do to track her down. She needs to be notified as next of kin, which I'll do personally, but find her for me."

Brown nodded and took the bag. "Sir, do we know if she's in this state?"

"She should be local. According to Ms. Hannah, he stayed close to be near his daughter."

"Got it." Brown turned and left.

Dawson headed back toward the conference room. As he entered, he noticed Hannah sleeping peacefully in the corner, so he backed out and shut the door quietly. He left a sticky note on the door stating it was being used, then asked a female officer to keep an eye out for Ms. Hannah when she woke up. He also left a few dollars for the officer to buy a sandwich for the woman to eat before leaving the station.

Dawson moved from the precinct, and went across the street to the coroner's office. He took a deep breath and started down that blasted sterile hall to find Jenson. He entered her office and glanced around at the utter disarray. Charts and files were everywhere.

"Welcome to my chaos." The soft voice behind him startled him.

He turned to face her and took in her dark hair pulled back in a ponytail. She wore very little makeup, with just a hint of mascara lining her eyelashes.

"Just thought I'd stop by and see if you had any other information on our John Doe."

"Still running some tests. Obvious cause of death—blunt force trauma to the face and head. No information on dental records." She moved around Dawson and cleared away the files that were piled in the chair next to her desk. Placing them on another stack on the already crowded desk, she nodded for him to sit as she slid into her own chair.

"We may have a name. Still trying to locate the next of kin…Eugene Henry."

Jenson nodded and sat back. Dawson glanced around again, avoiding eye contact.

"Was there something else on your mind?" she finally said.

"No, not really." He looked at her, feeling foolish for his lack of response.

"Want to tell me what your soft spot is with the homeless?"

"I don't have a soft spot for the homeless." He stood, ready to be on the defensive, hands clenched at his side. "What gives you that impression?"

"Whoa, wait a minute. It's not a bad thing." Jenson got up and placed a hand on his arm. "I actually find it quite refreshing."

He let out a long sigh. "Sorry. It's a tough case, and I don't particularly like treating someone like they're no one just because they don't have any family or a home to live in."

Jenson nodded. The heat from her hand penetrated through to Dawson and he covered it with his other hand. He sat back down. After a moment, he met her eyes. She gave him a smile, encouraging him to continue.

"Look, we don't know each other that well. I just…" He broke off and shrugged.

"I'm Ali. Allison actually, but I prefer Ali."

"Wesley. Wes."

Ali sat back down. "Well, now we know each other a bit better. Being on a first-name basis with someone really makes you friends."

Dawson laughed out loud. "I like the way you think."

"So, tell me about the homeless soft spot. I, too, have one and there are very few of us."

He closed his eyes. "My sister ran away from home years ago. She's out there on the streets somewhere. Every time I come across a homeless person, I feel it could be her."

Ali nodded. "I get it. I don't have a direct involvement like you do, I just wish I could do more to help."

"I hear from her every couple of years. A small note stuck in my door. She knows where I live, although I don't know how. Why would she continue to stay on the streets?"

Ali leaned forward, took his hands in hers, and squeezed. "We can't always know the reasoning of someone else. But, at least, she reaches out to you every so often."

Dawson locked his eyes with hers. They were such a dark brown, chocolate color, and so full of sincerity. He was mesmerized and wanted to lean forward to kiss her. Instead, he shook his head to clear the thought. "I should go."

He stood to leave and hesitated briefly at the door when he heard her voice. "Dawson, I'm here if you want to talk."

He nodded without turning around and left the office.

Ali watched Dawson leave the office. She took a deep breath and exhaled slowly. Since when did a man affect her the way this one did? She'd been drawn to him and had ached when she'd touched him briefly. An ache that she hadn't felt in years. She had watched him talk about his sister and her heart ached for him. She'd wanted to pull him into her arms and just hold him...well, and kiss away the hurt and pain he was feeling.

She shook her head. This train of thought was going nowhere and could only lead to dangerous behavior. They were professionals and it had to stay that way.

But oh, he looked sexy as hell when he was brooding.

six

Dawson had no sooner stepped outside of the Medical Examiner's office onto the street when his cell phone vibrated. *Another one – West St alley halfway down the block.* The text sent a chill up his spine as he turned toward the precinct. Since he'd walked to the station today, he'd grab a ride with another officer.

Even though he arrived at the scene within fifteen minutes of receiving the text, the place was already crawling with reporters. He ducked under the yellow tape lining the perimeter and found Officer Brown taking pictures of the scene.

He moved close to Brown. "Whatcha got?"

"Same type of weapon it looks like. Victim is female this time. No ID on her."

Dawson nodded and glanced around the victim. A pool of blood circled her head, and her face had been sliced beyond recognition like the other case. Blood spatter was far-reaching this time, indicative of rage on the part of the killer. "Have you canvassed the area yet? Looked in dumpsters for a purse or anything?"

Brown nodded. "Couple uniforms are on it."

"Damn. Perp really likes to mutilate their faces, huh?"

Brown glanced at the victim. "Not a pretty sight, that's for sure."

Dawson expanded his view as he stepped away from the body, glancing in all directions. "Any witnesses?"

"The kid over there found her." Brown gestured with his head to a young boy talking with another police officer.

Dawson approached them. He nodded to the officer who stepped back, allowing Dawson to get closer to the boy.

"My name's Wes. And you are?" Dawson leaned against the wall. The boy was nervous, but followed Dawson's lead and mimicked his stance.

"Billy. I didn't do anything."

"I didn't think you did, Son. Why would you immediately jump to that?"

"Cops around here always blame the kid."

Dawson nodded. "Are you on the streets a lot?"

"Some. My mom works down the street. She tells me to stay out of trouble, and I try to."

"Did you see what happened to the lady over there?"

Billy shook his head. "She was lying there when I came around the corner. I ran back down to Mom's work and called the cops."

Dawson studied the boy. His posture slumped forward but he appeared to be telling the truth. The child was dirty and probably hungry. "Have you eaten today?"

"Yeah. My mom feeds me." The boy scowled and fisted his hands beside him.

Dawson held up his hand. "Not trying to offend you, Son. Just wondered if you were hungry." Dawson met Billy's eyes. The boy was tense and obviously nervous.

"No, sir. My mom and I will eat dinner later."

"Suit yourself. Did you give the officer your name and how to reach you…in case I have more questions?"

Billy nodded. "My mom did when he asked to talk to me. Can I go now?" He glanced over at the body lying in the pool of blood.

"Yeah, go ahead." Dawson watched the boy run down

the alleyway. Another hungry child. Was the victim another homeless person? She wasn't dressed like she was homeless, but to be found in the alley, one had to wonder who she was and what she was doing there.

Dawson made his way further into the alley, keeping his eyes on the ground and taking in every little thing. The filth was heavy here. Dumpsters were overflowing and the stench got stronger and stronger the deeper into the alley he went. Nothing looked out of place, if you found the filth to be in place. Dawson kept his breathing shallow, trying to limit what he inhaled.

He met a couple of uniformed officers coming toward him. "Nothing here."

Dawson stopped in front of them. "You checked all the dumpsters?"

Both men glanced at each other before looking back to him. "We looked in them, yes. Nothing could be seen."

Dawson stared at them. "So, you basically just glanced at the top of the garbage, and if anything was placed in there lately, you couldn't see anything beneath it? Is that what you're telling me?"

"Well, sir…"

Dawson held up his hand. "You better hope nothing is in there, or I'm coming after you both for missing it."

Both officers nodded. "We'll do another sweep."

Dawson grinned as they walked away. He remembered all too well the days where detectives stuck rookie uniforms on the crappy aspects of an investigation. Dawson turned and strode toward the main road. As he came into view of the victim again, he stopped. Jenson had arrived, and she was bent over the body.

"Jenson, whatcha got?"

She glanced up. "Pretty much the same. Obviously, the same weapon that killed Eugene. I would say time of death was between eleven and midnight."

Dawson frowned.

"Hopefully, I'll know more once I get her back to the morgue and do a little more digging." She stood and pulled off her latex gloves. "Are we looking at another homeless victim?"

He gestured for her to move to the side away from everyone. "I hope not, but I don't have any information on who she is."

Ali looked up at him warily. "Can you be sure it's not your sister?"

"Too tall for her." Dawson cringed at his own gruffness, but he softened when Ali laid her hand on his arm and gently squeezed.

"I'll let you know what I find out."

He nodded as she walked off toward the medical-examiner van. The body had been loaded and her time at the crime scene was done. He couldn't help but feel a sense of loss as the vehicle drove away.

As Ali drove back to the morgue with the body, her mind wandered. There was a bond that seemed to be growing between Ali and Dawson. From what she knew of Dawson, he struck her as the type of man who'd keep his personal matters to himself, and she felt honored that he felt comfortable enough to talk to her about Sara.

These crimes were definitely different, or maybe the difference Ali was feeling was due to dealing with Dawson instead of a local guy who acted like she didn't have a brain in her head.

Dawson showed her respect, and Ali reciprocated it with ease.

Was it only respect she was feeling for him?

She'd been trying to fight the way he crept into her mind while she was working, and how her thoughts would wander when she sat down to do paperwork. The path her mind took always ended with Dawson and some very unprofessional thoughts.

Not that she wanted to be called to crime scenes for yet another dead body, but the tingle that went through her at the thought of seeing Dawson there made her realize he was more to her than just a coworker.

She sighed. How long could she fight these feelings, or, at least, keep them from him?

seven

Dawson made another pot of coffee. He'd spent the night at the local precinct at his temporary desk, pouring over the report that Jenson had given him regarding Eugene. There was no real information in it that pointed him in any specific direction.

Frustrated, Dawson ran his fingers through his thick hair. The gesture left it standing upright, surely making him look every bit the unkempt man he felt.

"Did you get any sleep at all?"

Dawson turned slowly to meet Ali's eyes. He shook his head. "Coffee?"

"Sure, I'll have a cup. Although I think you could stand to actually get some food in you." She reached for the cup in his hand and placed it on the counter where the coffee pot brewed. "Have you eaten at all?"

"No. Haven't had time." He shrugged.

"Well, come on. Let's hit the diner down the street. They have the best omelets, and we can talk about our newest victim."

"Great, just don't put ketchup on your omelet."

Ali's laughter filled the station. Dawson smiled, letting his guard slip just a little. They walked in silence to the diner. He looked up and was surprised that this was the location across from the first crime scene. Ali nodded when she saw his recognition.

They entered and found a quiet booth near the back where they perused their menu and waited for Beth to wait on them.

"What can I getcha?" Beth never made eye contact.

"Hi, Beth. Remember me? Detective Dawson?"

She nodded and slowly raised her eyes to meet his. "What can I getcha?" she repeated in monotone.

Dawson tapped on the menu. "Fully loaded meat omelet, wheat toast, and home fries."

Ali smiled. "Veggie omelet, wheat toast, and home fries for me. Thanks."

Beth nodded, and without another word, left the table.

"Well, she's a treat to chat with," Ali said while looking around the diner.

Dawson followed her gaze. The place was about half full, and obviously, the people who were at the tables were regulars. There was no other wait staff except for Beth, who was trying very hard to avoid most of her customers. The crude comments about her being lazy filled the diner as people requested coffee and didn't get it.

"I've been here a lot and have never seen such a circus," Ali went on. "Usually, there's another waitress, Amy, who's right on top of things."

"Owner told me she's been out sick for a few days. He thinks she actually quit but didn't have the balls to tell him."

Ali looked Dawson in the eyes. "Did you follow up with her?"

"I'm headed there today. Got a little sidetracked yesterday with the new victim."

Beth appeared next to the table and slid plates in front of each of them. "Anything else?"

"Beth, has Amy been back to work yet?"

"Nope."

Dawson stared hard at her, her discomfort palpable in the air around them.

"Anything else?" She gritted her teeth, giving the words a snarl as they came out. Her stance was already turned as if she was ready to bolt.

"More coffee, please, while you're filling up the others who are asking."

The glare Beth shot Dawson as she walked away had him snickering until Ali interrupted him. "Why bait her?"

"There's something about her. I can't put my finger on it."

"She's an introvert and is here only because the owner is family. It's obviously not a job that she's comfortable in."

He bit into his omelet. "If you say so."

"Your mind thinks the worst of everyone, doesn't it?"

Laughter overtook him, and he choked as he swallowed his bite of omelet. Coughing, he took a sip of coffee. "I don't think the worst of you." He winked at Ali.

"Good, because you're buying breakfast."

They ate in silence until Ali pushed her plate away. "So, I did the autopsy on the new victim. Had dental records run." Dawson nodded. "Local lady named Darla Johnson."

"Do we know anything else about her?"

Ali shook her head. "I wanted to tell you first. I figured you'd want to track down her family yourself."

He nodded. "Thanks."

Ali reached across the table and held his hand. "I'm sure you'll find family for the vic. Keep reminding yourself, it's not Sara."

"It's funny. I never stop searching for her, but she keeps just out of reach. I don't get *why?*" He squeezed her hand, then pulled his back. He couldn't let himself get involved, no matter how attractive Ali was and how much he felt a connection with her. He refused to look up and meet her eyes, knowing he'd probably see hurt in them for pulling away. She was just one more person he'd let down.

"Well, we should get to it." He threw some money on the table, stood, and waited for Ali to stand, then followed her out.

Dawson walked beside her all the way back to the precinct, lost in his own thoughts. He felt like a heel for shutting her down, but he couldn't handle the emotions flowing through him. From the pain he still felt from losing his sister, to the sadness that overwhelmed him, and the guilt in not being able to find her. Ali's compassion just intensified every emotion, and he felt so ill-equipped to deal with it.

She stopped on the steps of the precinct. "I've got work to do. Thanks for breakfast."

He studied her face. "You're welcome."

She hesitated for a moment, then gave him a small smile. "I'm sure we'll be talking."

He watched her walk away and couldn't help but feel a small pang of loss. He'd no sooner walked through the door when the captain yelled for him. Maybe it was a good thing. He'd been given no time to wallow.

He strolled into the captain's office and sank into the chair. "What can I do for you?"

"Really? Where are we on this homeless guy's murder? I've got the press bugging me for a statement."

"There's been another victim. We've identified the homeless guy, Eugene Henry, and we're trying to reach his daughter now."

"And the new victim?"

"Woman named Darla Johnson. I'm trying to locate her family now, too."

Collins stood. "By sitting here?"

Dawson shook his head and left the office. He started for his desk when his cell phone vibrated. A number he

didn't recognize was coming in, but he answered it anyway. "Dawson."

The silence was deafening.

He decided to try again. "Hello?"

A beep indicated the call had ended. Sputtering under his breath, he dropped the phone on his desk and slid
into the chair. He didn't have time for this. He picked up
the phone again and pulled up the call log. Staring at the
number, he wondered who it was. Was it related to the
murders?

"Brown!"

"Yes, sir?" Brown crossed the room quickly.

"Trace this number for me." Dawson pulled a notepad
from his pocket and scribbled it down before tearing off
the page and handing it to the rookie. "Where are we on
notifying next of kin?"

"Still trying to find an address on Henry's daughter."

"Damn it. She can't be that hard to find." Dawson
ran his fingers through his hair in frustration. A habit he
couldn't break. "We need to move forward on this, not
just stand around doing nothing."

"Yes, sir." Brown turned toward his desk.

Dawson knew he was being a prick, but his frustration level was high and he wanted to get this case solved.
There was no way he wanted a third victim to come
across his desk. He closed his eyes, trying to stop the
headache that was starting. He wasn't sleeping and stress
was high. The local captain was going to be up his ass on
this case until it was solved, as well as his own boss, and
he couldn't afford to screw this up.

"Sir?"

Dawson opened his eyes and found Brown standing
in front of him. "Tell me you have something for me."

"Nothing on the number. It's a prepaid."

"Damn it." Dawson pushed his chair back and stood.
Brown stepped aside nervously and waited. "Find me the

address for Eugene's daughter. I want something!" He barked out the order as he headed for the door. "Text me the information and I want it yesterday, Brown!"

"Yes, sir."

With his mind reeling, Dawson left the precinct and started down the street. His gut was telling him to be prepared for more fallout.

He stopped at a street vendor and bought a bottled water, and as he continued walking, his mind replayed the murder scene of the first victim. He could see clearly the blood and the body. What he couldn't place was any insight to the killer. They couldn't get a fix on height. His preliminary profile assumed a male, because of the force of the blows to the victim's face, someone who was a decent height and build, judging by the pattern of blood spatter.

Dawson sighed and glanced around him. He was in front of the still-taped-off alley of the first victim. He ducked under the tape and walked toward the scene. Blood was dried on the ground. Aside from that, one would never know something had happened here. The ground was still filthy and everything was back to being a normal alley with trash littered around.

He circled the bloodstain and tried to envision the scene. His mind was blank and the frustration built once more.

His phone vibrated and he pulled it out. Glancing at the text, he saw Katie's address, the daughter of the first victim. He scowled, as he knew this was going to be a difficult conversation. He recognized the address as being just a couple of blocks north, and he walked with purpose in that direction. How ironic was it that her father was squatting so close to where she lived? Did he know his daughter was right there, nearby? Did she know her father had been living on the streets and not just *any* streets, but the ones in her neighborhood?

His heart ached, once more, for his sister who was somewhere out there. Did she stay close to him to make it easier for her? Why wouldn't she reach out to him and allow him to help her?

He sighed and squared his shoulders. Fuck the sentimentality of all of it. If that was the way his sister wanted it to be, he could harden his heart just like his parents had done. He swore under his breath, knowing that they were just words of frustration, and deep down, he wanted nothing more than to take his sister in his arms and let her know he'd always be there for her.

eight

Dawson paused at the steps of the brownstone. These were the moments he dreaded as a detective. Telling the family that they'd lost a family member was hard. He sympathized with them, but had to maintain an emotionless presence.

He took the steps slowly and rang the doorbell. He could hear footsteps inside. As he waited for someone to open the door, he glanced around. It was a nice neighborhood, so different than the one just two blocks away where Eugene had been living in the alley.

Dawson sadly shook his head and faced the door as the handle turned.

"Can I help you?" A pair of bright blue eyes peered out. She'd only opened the door wide enough to look out, and Dawson couldn't see past her.

"I'm looking for Katie Henry." He showed his badge and waited.

"I used to be Katie Henry." She glanced over her shoulder, but provided no further information.

"Katie…" Dawson hated being so informal with her,

but she clearly didn't want her married name known. "You're the daughter of Eugene Henry?"

She nodded.

"When was the last time you saw your father?" Dawson was stalling, but he couldn't read this woman. She was practically hidden behind the door.

"I haven't spoken to him in years. Look, if you're searching for him, I couldn't tell you where he is." She started to close the door, and Dawson reached out a hand to stop it.

"Miss, I really need to speak with you. May I come in?"

She stared at him for a moment before shaking her head. "I prefer you didn't. What is it you need to say?"

"It's about your dad."

"So, say it." She glanced over her shoulder again and shut the door just a fraction more.

"Katie, who's at the door?" a male voice behind her bellowed out.

"A police officer looking for someone. No one we know." She shook her head at Dawson. "Please, not now," she whispered and shut the door.

Dawson stood there staring at the closed door before him, unable to turn and walk down the steps. Obviously, she didn't want to know about her father, but Dawson was determined she learned what was going on.

He turned his back to the brownstone and looked around. The street was quiet. Not much traffic. In fact, it was almost too quiet. He slowly descended the stairs and crossed the road. Moving down the sidewalk, he positioned himself about three doors down and sat on an empty stoop, just watching Katie's door.

He had a feeling he'd been watched as he left and only hoped Katie would come out that door. He pulled his phone from his pocket and pretended to be reading a text as he sat there and waited. It didn't take long before

Katie exited the building. She peeked over at him, then walked in the other direction.

He glanced up at the brownstone and saw a man standing in the window watching her walk away. The man never looked in his direction, so Dawson stayed where he was. Once Katie reached the corner and went out of sight, the man dropped the curtain and moved away from the window.

Dawson stood and crossed the street, heading away from the direction Katie took. He went down the next side street and doubled back to the street where Katie had gone. She was standing in a doorway with her arms crossed, obviously waiting for him.

"What is it you want?" she whispered as he got close to her.

"Is there someplace we can talk?" Dawson was guarded with her behavior.

"Tell me what you have to. I don't have much time. I'm headed to the store to get milk." She gestured to the convenience store across the street.

"I'll walk with you over there."

"No. I can't be seen with you."

Dawson stared at her. "Why? Who is the man watching you?"

She shrugged. "My husband worries about me."

"Katie, if he's hurting you, I can help…"

She shook her head. "Please. Don't make this harder. What about my father?"

Dawson sighed. "He was killed the other night. I tracked you down to let you know."

Her eyes grew wide and tears threatened to spill over. "Where?"

"Just a few blocks from here. Did you know he was living on the street?"

She nodded. "I wanted to help him, but…"

"But your husband didn't know he was homeless?"

"My husband *put* him on the street." Katie wiped away a lone tear that escaped as she blinked back others that were ready to fall. "Please. I can't talk about this." She turned toward the store.

Dawson held out his card. "Call me night or day for anything. You'll need to make arrangements for your father."

She grabbed the card and simply nodded. "I'll be in touch." She turned and almost sprinted across the street.

He could only stand there and watch her go. This had certainly not gone as expected. He stayed right where he was until Katie had come out with her milk and headed home, then he shook his head and turned back toward the station. He needed to figure out just exactly who this husband was and why he had such a hold on her. She was running scared like an abused woman, and Dawson had no tolerance for that kind of behavior.

He called Brown on his walk to the station. "I need to find out Katie Henry's married name and who her husband is. Get whatever information you can find. I'll be back shortly and I'll want what you have."

"Sir, it may take a little time."

"There is no time. Just have it ready for me." Dawson disconnected the call before the rookie could respond and slipped his phone in his pocket. He arrived back at the precinct just as Brown was headed out the door.

"What do you have?"

Brown handed him a file. "Jenson called, wants to see you. Said your cell phone kept going to voice mail."

"Impossible." Dawson pulled out his phone. The battery was dead. Damn it. Not the time he needed his battery to go on the fritz. "I'll head her way. Did she say why?"

"Vic two's family is coming to ID the body. She wants you there."

"Got it." Dawson turned and started a jog toward the ME's office. This day just couldn't get any better. He needed a break soon.

He arrived at the ME's office just as an older man was entering. Dawson slipped passed him as he checked in, then headed down the hall to Ali's office, wanting to speak with her before the family got there.

"Hey, sorry about the phone. Battery died."

Ali pointed at a charger on her desk. "Go ahead and see how much charge you can get while you're here."

"Thanks. What's the word?"

"Family was instructed to come ID. I thought you were going to go speak with them?"

He shook his head. "I went to speak with the daughter from the first victim. There's something going on there. I sent Brown to talk to this family."

Ali's intercom buzzed and a voice announced that Darla Johnson's family was on their way down to the morgue. Ali acknowledged it and turned to Dawson.

"You okay?"

He nodded and gestured for her to precede him out of the office. They arrived in front of the morgue doors just as the older man entered the hallway outside the morgue. Ali approached him. "Mr. Johnson?"

"Yes. Is my daughter here?"

"Come this way. This is Detective Dawson, sir."

Dawson shook the man's hand. "I'm sorry for your loss, sir."

"Well, let's hope it's not her."

Dawson put his hand on the man's shoulder. "Sir, were you told that her face was unrecognizable?"

"Yes, that's what they said. But I'd know her by her jewelry. She wears one of her momma's rings, and unless it was stolen, I'll know her."

Ali nodded.

Dawson raised a hand to signal Ali to wait. "Why don't we just show you her hands then, sir?"

Ali acknowledged the tactic and looked to the elderly gentleman for his agreement. The man nodded slowly, his uncertainty clearly showing through. Ali pulled the side of the sheet back exposing the right hand of the victim. No rings.

"It would be on her *left* hand," the man said. "She wore it on her ring finger after she was divorced."

Ali nodded and dropped the sheet back over the right hand. She moved around the table and pulled away the covering to reveal the left hand. On her ring finger was an amethyst ring.

The man nodded as tears flooded his eyes and poured down his cheeks. "My girl…"

Dawson kept a grip on the man's shoulder, feeling the shudders of sobs racking the man's body. He wanted to assure him it would be all right, but he couldn't find the words with no hope, at the moment, of catching the killer.

The man reached up and patted his hand. "Catch whoever did this, Son."

"I intend to, sir." Dawson stepped away with Ali to the side of the room and allowed the man to hold the hand of his daughter, now gone.

"She was all I had left." The man kissed his daughter's hand and gently placed the sheet back over it. He turned and faced them. "When can I take her and allow her to rest peacefully?"

"Have your funeral director contact us, and we'll release the body." Ali walked over and slid the ring off Darla's finger, then placed it in the father's hand. He simply nodded and walked out.

"I hate days like this." Ali moved to her office and sat down at the desk.

Dawson leaned against the doorframe and watched her. "I hear ya. It never seems to get easier."

"Do you want to talk about your earlier visit with the daughter of the first victim?"

He shook his head, but came into the room and sat down. He picked up the folder he'd dropped on the desk next to his phone. Flipping through it, he discovered there wasn't a lot of information. The name of Katie's husband was a surprise. Big politician in the city. The file contained investments that he had recently picked up and one was showing that it had been an apartment building with controlled rent for elderly people. Most had been displaced onto the streets, as they had nowhere else to go.

Dawson's anger grew the more he read, and he threw the file on the desk in front of Ali in disgust. "There's something wrong with this, and yet, some people seem to be able to live just outside of the law."

Ali picked up the file and started reading. He watched her, satisfied to see she was as shocked and dismayed as he was.

"This is Eugene's son-in-law?" she asked.

Dawson smiled at her use of the victim's first name. This fight had just become personal for the two of them. He, at least, was not alone in the battle.

"I don't know what to do. Katie wouldn't really talk with me." He went on to explain about their meeting and how scared she was to be seen with him.

"There's not much you can do," Ali said softly, "except wait for her to come to you."

Dawson grunted. He checked his phone for the battery level, then sat back and waited.

Ali's quiet laugh brought his eyes up to meet hers. "You know I'm right and you just don't want to admit it."

"It goes against my grain to sit back and wait for something bad to happen. My gut tells me she could be in danger, and yet, I have to sit around and do nothing. It's not right."

Ali reached out and grabbed his hand. "No, it's not, but sometimes our hands are tied, and that's all *we* can do."

He ran his thumb over her palm. Her skin was as soft as her voice, and he just wanted to pull her close to him. Instead, he drew away. He couldn't go there. His focus had to be the case.

He grabbed his phone and unplugged it. "I've got enough juice for now. I'll talk to you later."

He picked up the folder and moved toward the door. Ali's quiet "bye" lingered as he headed out of her office. He'd acted like a jerk, but he couldn't help it. This wasn't what he needed in his life right now.

Dawson's abrupt departure stung.

Ali tried to reason with herself that he was just upset and frustrated, but for some reason it hurt. She knew she was getting too invested in this, in him, but she's come to the realization that she couldn't fight her feelings. She was tired of pushing the emotions away and being stoic. She wanted to be strong for Dawson, yes, but in return she wanted him to hold her and let her know that all this was going to be okay.

This case was wearing on both of them, and they each had very different ways of dealing with the stress of it. Dawson's MO apparently was to push her aside and act like the bulldog who couldn't see anything but the bone in front of him, even if it was out of reach.

She sighed. She'd granted herself permission to accept her feelings for him, but that didn't mean she needed to act on them. But the sadness that filled his eyes when he talked of Sara tugged at her heart strings.

And his touch…

For a moment, he'd caressed her briefly with his thumb, and the heat that shot through her was unnerving. There was no doubt she wanted the man, and she was walking a fine line between sanity and insanity whenever he was near her.

nine

Dawson arrived home, needing to clear his mind and really think. He changed into shorts and headed to his garage. His punching bag hung from the ceiling in the center of the room. He started with roundhouse kicks, slowly and methodically placing each one. As he progressed through his workout, his frustration came to a head and each kick came with more force.

The ringing of his phone brought him to a stop, and as he glanced at the clock, he realized he'd been working out for almost an hour. "Dawson," he answered.

"I need to talk to you." A female voice came through.

"Who is this?"

"Katie."

"Can you meet me at the station?"

"No." There was silence.

"Okay, meet me at the diner at Fifth and Main Street." He waited for her response for what seemed like forever.

"I'll be there in a half hour." The phone disconnected.

Dawson glanced down at the time. He had just

enough time to take a quick shower and get there before she did. He didn't want her to have to wait and chicken out on talking with him.

He arrived with five minutes to spare. Peering around, he noticed Beth working. Seemed she never had a day off. He planned on that to work in his favor since she probably wouldn't come to the table to check on them. He sat there waiting, watching the time, and didn't realize he was so anxious until he saw Katie walk in. He raised his hand to get her attention and motioned for her to join him.

Beth appeared at the table. "What can I get you?"

"Just coffee for me," Katie answered.

"Same here."

The waitress walked away. Dawson stayed quiet, allowing Katie to gather her thoughts. She played with a napkin and never met his eyes. They sat without speaking, until their coffee had been placed in front of them.

"I don't know if I can make arrangements for Dad," Katie finally said. "I can't have a service for him."

Dawson struggled to keep the shock from his face. "Why? He deserves some sort of remembrance."

Katie met Dawson's gaze. Her eyes showed unshed tears. "My husband doesn't think it'll be good for his career to have our name associated with a homeless man."

"Damn." Dawson took a deep breath. "You know he displaced your father and forced him into *being* a homeless person. What kind of grip does he have on you that you can't even mourn the death of a parent?"

Dawson felt like he'd been sucker-punched when Katie's tears started flowing unchecked. "I just can't."

He pushed his unused napkin toward her. "Katie, tell me what's going on? It's more than just keeping up appearances."

She wiped her tears away and struggled to compose herself. "Detective Dawson, I really appreciate your concern, but everything is fine."

He held back the sharp retort and finished his coffee. "I'm available anytime, Katie. But we need to know what to do with your dad. How are we going to honor his life?"

Katie froze. "*We?*"

"You don't need to do this alone. I'll help, but Eugene deserves better than to be just brushed aside like a nobody. He was your father. Have you no memories as a child of this man in your life?"

She nodded. "He was a good father. I had a great childhood. We lost touch after momma died, but he was doing okay until Finn took over the apartment complex he lived in. Once he was evicted, I couldn't do anything. I tried to slip him some money every now and again, but it wasn't easy."

Dawson waited, listening.

"He never treated me with resentment, but how could he possibly not be resentful when his only daughter just left him on the streets?" The anguish in her voice tore at Dawson.

"Let me help you set something up to honor him, even if it's just a graveside service. He had a lot of friends on the street and he's greatly missed." He kept his voice soft, almost a whisper. He ached for his sister who was somewhere unknown on the streets, and he couldn't imagine if his parents wouldn't step up and honor her if something happened to her.

"I'll call you. I'll try to get some money put away to get to you. If you can handle the details, I'll be there that day."

He nodded as she slipped out of the booth. "Keep my number, Katie...I mean it. I'm available anytime."

She whispered, "Thanks," as she headed to the door.

Dawson sat back and pondered the conversation. He knew he was in trouble if the captain got wind that he was going to help plan a memorial for the first victim. His glance wandered to Beth, standing behind the counter ignoring the customers still left in the diner. He couldn't imagine she was getting very good tips at all with her lack of customer service. She looked so broken and beaten down. He needed to reach Amy, the other waitress, and get some insight to Beth's story. Or at least find out why Amy conveniently disappeared just as the killing happened.

He sighed as he stood. He threw some money down on the table—more than he should have—but he couldn't help but feel sorry for Beth. She may be a bad waitress, but the customers were just plain cruel to her.

Ten

After he returned home last night, Dawson had spent the next couple hours working out with his punching bag, before finally falling into a restless sleep. The frustration never seemed to wane, but at least he was in good shape. He smirked at the thought and waited for his coffee to brew. It was going to be a long day. He prayed Brown had some good news for him.

He keyed in a text to Ali asking her to meet him outside the precinct in twenty minutes. He needed to run the situation with Katie by her. Maybe she could help with the memorial service for Eugene and keep him out of the line of fire from his boss.

Dawson closed his eyes and willed the start of a headache from becoming full blown. Pinching the bridge of his nose, he inhaled slowly. The fresh-brewed coffee assaulted his senses, and he reached for his travel mug to fill.

He walked briskly as he sipped his coffee, his mind running away and going in a hundred different directions. He paused when he saw Ali sitting on the steps outside the station and watched her study her phone before starting toward her.

"Hey."

She shielded her eyes as she glanced up at him. "Hey yourself."

He sat down beside her. "I need to run something by you ... I know it's crazy, but..." He took a long drink of his coffee, then sat in silence.

"But?"

He could feel her smiling, even before he looked at her. "Katie called me last night to meet her. We met for coffee." He paused, giving Ali a chance to jump in. Since she made no remark, he continued. "She didn't want to do anything for her father. Nothing."

"Didn't want to? And now?"

Dawson nodded. "I may have guilted her into it. She asked if I could help. For some reason, she doesn't want her husband to know."

"Well, you had a feeling there was more going on there. Did she give any indication of what it was?"

He shook his head. "Just that it would look bad to have a homeless man linked to their name." They sat in silence. He struggled with words as anger consumed him. "How could she do that?"

"What you really mean is, would your family do the same if it was Sara." It wasn't a question, just a simple statement that hit him hard.

"I wouldn't. I would honor her and her life." He could feel Ali's eyes on him, and he just wanted the ground to open up and consume him. He couldn't run from the shameful things his parents had done.

"It's a different situation, Wes." Her soft voice cut through his thoughts.

"I know." He faced her directly. "But what does her husband have over her that she could turn her back on her father? She admits she had a great childhood with him."

"Wes, you know as well as I do that you can't anticipate what someone will do. There's always more to a person's situation than meets the eye, especially if they're trying to hide it."

The truth was, Dawson knew that better than anyone. He hated feeling so helpless. "So, I wait for Katie to contact me again."

Ali stood and reached out to help him up. "Yup. Is this all you needed? Or do you want me to start looking into what we can do to honor Eugene that would be simple? Something that we could get the word on the street to his homeless friends?"

Dawson smiled. "How do you know me so well?"

Ali scoffed. "As much as you like to think you're a mystery, you're an open book." She waved a hand up in the air as she started to walk off. "I'll take care of it."

"You're the best!" he called out after her.

He took the steps two at a time to get inside the station. Ali always lifted his mood. He caught sight of Brown sitting at his desk, talking on the phone.

Dawson went into the conference room where he'd set up his victimology board to study it. So far, there were no connections between the two. Eugene had been homeless, thanks to his son-in-law. With no other reason than not wanting a homeless man associated with his name, Finn O'Shannahan seemed to be the only one who would want him out of the way. Katie didn't seem to have any insight as to her father or her husband—at least, that she wanted to share.

He turned his attention to victim two, Darla. They hadn't dug up too much on her yet, other than having an ex-husband who was in jail for domestic violence and almost killing her. No word from Brown yet as to where the man was in his sentence. She was a quiet woman, who'd just recently achieved her real estate license. So far, she hadn't been working in that field long enough to piss off anyone.

Dawson looked between the pictures of his two victims. There was no connection between them that he could find.

He turned with a start when the door to the conference room opened.

"Sir, I might have something for you."

"Stop with the *sir*." Dawson barked. He spun around to see Brown hesitating in the doorway. "Get in here."

Brown stepped into the room, then glanced at the board, and back to Dawson. "Vic two's ex was released from prison last week."

"What? Was his sentence up?" Dawson reached for the papers Brown was holding.

"Early parole for good behavior." Brown handed him everything.

"Do we know where he is now?"

"Holed up in a sleazy apartment complex on Sixth Street."

"Bring him in." Dawson turned back toward the board. "ASAP, Brown."

"Yes, sir." Brown was out the door before Dawson could protest the title.

Interesting turn of events, but still nothing that linked the two victims together. Dawson pinned up a picture of Darla's ex under her, before he turned to go over the arrest report handed to him. Numerous domestic disputes had been reported at the victim's house and had escalated, but she never pressed charges until a year ago when he was caught with his hands around her throat. Because she finally took legal action against him, he'd been put away. The ex had originally been handed down a sentence of two years, but apparently, he got one year and was let out.

Disgust boiled up in Dawson. Another imperfection in the justice system. A man is released, and his ex-wife ends up dead within days of his departure from prison.

eleven

Dawson stared at the victimology board. He raked his fingers through his hair, frustration oozing from him. He needed a break soon in this case. Not only did he want to get back to his own office, but the Leighton captain was breathing down his back, and he couldn't be hand-holding Brown at every turn.

Dawson shook his head at the thought of Brown jumping every time he spoke. True enough, Dawson wasn't the gentlest person, and he was often too harsh with others, but Brown needed to relax and stop being so damn kiss-ass. Dawson was a perfectionist through and through, and it grated on him to not have a good grasp of the details of these crimes.

"Sir?" Brown spoke from the door. "Carl Johnson is in interrogation room one." He was gone before Dawson could respond.

"I swear I'll kill him if he calls me sir one more time," Dawson mumbled under his breath as he made his way to the room where Mr. Johnson waited.

Before going in, Dawson stood outside the door and looked in through its window. The man sat, stiff-backed and rigid in the chair, hands clasped in front of him on the table. Dawson glanced down at the photos he'd brought with him to show the guy. Pictures of Darla, unrecognizable with her face mutilated by the blade the killer had wielded.

Dawson opened the door, stepped in, and closed the door quietly behind him. No word was spoken as he walked the few steps over to the table and sat down across from Mr. Johnson.

"What am I here for?" The man's words were angry and the tone indicated the extent he was holding onto his rage. His clenched hands caused the veins in his arms to protrude up his tattooed arms. His black hair, cut short, matched the darkness of his eyes.

"Just a few questions for you," Dawson said.

"About what? I've kept to myself since getting out."

Dawson quietly laid out the photos in front of him. "What do you know about this?"

Carl studied the pictures. "Who is that?"

Dawson sat back in his chair with his arms crossed over his chest. "You don't know?"

Carl shook his head and continued to study the pictures. The man showed no emotion.

"Where were you on Tuesday night?" Dawson asked.

"At my apartment, probably. I go to work and go home." Carl looked up at Dawson. "Who is that?" he repeated with the same neutrality.

"Darla, your ex-wife." Dawson let the words sink in and could tell the moment the words penetrated, because Carl's eyes filled with tears and he looked at the pictures again.

Carl blinked hard, as if trying to stop his tears from spilling. He picked up the picture and looked at it closer, but shook his head. He swiped a lone tear that had escaped.

"Who would do that to her?" He pushed the pictures toward Dawson and swallowed hard—likely trying to control his emotions. "We had our issues, but I never wanted to kill her. In fact, I did a lot of thinking in prison, and I wanted to apologize to her. She was right for divorcing me, and I know that. I was ready to let her go. She deserved so much better than I ever gave her."

"That all sounds very good and noble, but the reality is you were in prison because of domestic violence, and shortly after you got out, your ex turns up dead."

"It wasn't me." His steel voice clipped.

"When was the last time you saw Darla?" Dawson changed tactics.

"I haven't had any contact with her. We haven't spoken since I was released." His hands shook, and Dawson saw the way he nervously clenched them together.

"No? But when was the last time you saw her, even if she didn't see you?" Dawson kept a straight face, but wanted to smirk at Carl's shocked expression.

"I never talked to her. I went to see her the other night, but didn't even end up knocking on her door."

"Why?"

"She had company, and I heard them arguing. I listened outside her door for a few minutes, then looked in her living room window to see if she was okay. She wasn't being hurt, and I knew I couldn't compete with the man that was in there, so I left."

Dawson held his gaze. "Who was the man?"

Carl shook his head. "Why should I tell you? What do I get out of it except a whole lot of trouble from him?"

"You'll get less trouble from me if we can verify your story."

Carl sat back and tapped his fingers on the table. The silence didn't bother Dawson, and he patiently waited. "That highfalutin politician in town. The one who's taking over all the buildings and tearing them down."

"O'Shannahan?"

He nodded. "Yup, that's his name."

Dawson gathered the pictures together and stood. "You're sure it was him at her place?"

"Yup."

Dawson turned and left the room, shutting the door behind him. "Brown!" he bellowed as he headed toward the office where they kept the victimology board.

"Yes, sir."

"Damn it, Brown. Knock off the sir crap." Dawson gestured for him to come in.

"What do you need, si … Detective?" Brown caught himself.

"We need to bring in Finn O'Shannahan and his wife, Katie, for questioning. I don't want them together when we do it." Dawson put the pictures in a folder. "I'll head over to their house now. Ride with me. Hopefully, there won't be any trouble, but I'd prefer if Katie—Mrs. O'Shannahan—follows us back here. She's not the one we're looking at."

Brown nodded and walked beside Dawson as they started for the car. "Why are we looking at Mr. O'Shanna-han? He was the first victim's father-in-law, but I thought there was no connection between the two victims."

Dawson smiled. "And here is where it gets interesting. Mr. Johnson went to see victim two, his ex, and found her with O'Shannahan. Coincidence? We will see."

Dawson pulled up in front of the O'Shannahan's brownstone. The window blinds were closed once again, no light showing from within. He gestured to Brown to follow him up the stone stairs, then gave a sharp rap to the knocker on the door and listened for sound inside.

The door cracked open, and Katie appeared. "Detective?"

"Who is it?" O'Shannahan yelled from the other room.

"Katie, I need to speak to him." She started to shake her head, but Dawson firmly pushed the door open.

"Finn, the police are here to see you." Katie backed up into the hallway as Dawson and Brown entered.

"Detective, what can I do for you?" Finn O'Shannahan was a large man, standing tall at around six feet four inches and a good 250 pounds, whose presence filled any space he was in. Although it was a narrow foyer, the largeness of Finn made it appear even smaller with hardly any room to walk past the desk against the wall.

Dawson, refusing to be intimidated by his size, took a step forward. "I need you to come to the station with me. We have some questions that we need to ask you."

"I'm sure you could ask me right here." The man stood, feet slightly apart, making his appearance even bigger as he engulfed the open area in the doorframe.

"Sir, I would prefer you come to the station. Mrs. O'Shannahan can follow us, so you can ride home with her." Dawson stepped to the side and gestured toward the door.

"What is this regarding?" Finn still hadn't moved, yet his stance stiffened in defiance.

Dawson took a deep breath, curbing his impatience. "I'd like to ask you some questions regarding the apartment building your father-in-law lived in before you tore it down." He felt Brown's eyes on him and briefly wondered if he was watching everything he did as a mentee or with disdain.

"I can't imagine what kind of questions you might have about that. It was a business deal." Finn crossed his arms over his chest.

"Sir, this doesn't have to be difficult, and I'm sure your wife doesn't need to be a part of this questioning." Dawson stared him down, until Finn nodded.

"Get the car, Katie, and meet us at the station. I'm sure I won't be long, so come right behind us."

Brown led the way to the car with Dawson following Finn. Dawson smiled and tried to convey reassurance to Katie who looked like a deer in headlights. Stopping at the car, Finn gaped at Brown as he opened the back door. "You surely don't expect me to ride in the back like a common criminal?"

Dawson stepped up. "Sir, it's standard procedure. You can't ride in the front, regardless of your position in the city."

With an exaggerated sigh, Finn slid into the back seat. Dawson, shaking his head at Brown, rolled his eyes as he went around the car to the driver's side. They rode in silence and arrived at the station.

When they exited the car, Dawson said, "Put him in room one, and I'll be there in a minute. I want to catch Katie and tell her what's going on. She can then be put in the break room so she'll be more comfortable."

Brown nodded. Opening the back door of the car, Dawson held back a sigh as Finn made an exaggerated move of getting out of the vehicle, grumbling how it was beneath him to ride in the back. "I'll be speaking to your captain about this."

Dawson turned on the steps. "I'll send him in to talk with you just as soon as I'm done." Dawson waited just inside the exterior door. He smirked as Brown tried to appease Finn while he led him down the corridor to the interrogation room.

Dawson typed a quick text to Ali: Katie at station. How's the plans going? When he finished, he watched for Katie and caught a glimpse of her parking the car. He stepped outside to wait for her on the steps.

"What is going on Detective Dawson?" She spoke before she even reached him.

"Just some questions for your husband, and I wanted to talk to you. My friend, Ali, the medical examiner, is helping plan the service for your dad." He opened the door for her and guided her through the bullpen to the break room. "Can I get you anything while you wait?" He gestured to the pot of coffee.

She shook her head. "Will I hear from your friend, or will you fill me in on the service details?"

Dawson's phone vibrated and he glanced down. Be there in a few to talk w/her. He smiled. Leave it to Ali to drop what she was doing to help. "She's on her way here. I'll let her know where you are, and she'll fill you in."

twelve

Dawson grabbed the folder of pictures before heading in to question Finn.

When Dawson entered the small expansion of the room, he found the man pacing.

"You have a lot of nerve keeping me waiting like this," Finn snarled.

Dawson didn't reply. He laid out two photographs of Eugene and another two of Darla, side by side on the wooden table. "Sir, do you know these people?"

Finn glared at him, but came over to the table and looked at the photos. "Are you mad? Their faces are destroyed. How would I know who they are?"

"Yes, they're cut up, but you know both of these people." Dawson paused, hoping for a reaction.

"You just asked me if I knew them, and now you're telling me I do. What kind of games does this department run? Where's the captain?"

Dawson gestured to the seat across from him. "Why don't you sit down? Captain Collins will be able to talk to you in a few minutes, and he can convey any complaints to my boss. But while we wait, why don't we get these questions out of the way?" Dawson waited until Finn settled himself in the hard metal chair, then he pointed to the pictures of Eugene. "This, sir, is your father-in-law, Eugene Henry."

Finn sat back in the chair, unfazed by the information. "I haven't seen that man in years. He had nothing to do with his daughter."

"He had nothing to do with his daughter? A man who carried around her picture with him and talked about her all the time? Interesting." Dawson paused. "This is the man you evicted from his apartment building so you could tear it down, giving no thought that your own father-in-law would be living on the streets. How did Katie take that news?"

Finn sat forward, glaring at Dawson. "*Mrs. O'Shannahan* didn't care that her father was on the streets. She had no relationship with him."

"That's the story you're staying with?" Dawson snarked.

"No story, it's simple truth." Finn pointed to the other two pictures. "And who is that?"

Dawson leaned back in his chair, watching Finn carefully. "Your lover."

Finn's face paled. "I don't know what you mean. I don't have a lover. Katie is the love of my life. How dare you!" He stood and started for the door.

"Sit down, Mr. O'Shannahan." Dawson didn't even look at him.

Finn stopped and turned. "I could have your job."

"You could, but you won't, since I'm doing my best to get a killer off the streets. Now sit and let's try again."

Finn slowly came back to the chair and plopped into it. "Try again? I told you the truth already."

Dawson shook his head. "When was the last time you saw Eugene?"

"Years ago. I don't know exactly. I haven't seen him since he was evicted."

"And your wife, when did she see her father last?"

Finn sighed. "I have no idea, but I would assume about the same time. She'd know better than to go against me and get in touch with him." The words slipped out, and Dawson saw the look of regret pass over Finn's face.

"Go against you? You didn't *allow* your wife to see her own father?" Dawson kept his tone neutral, struggling to maintain his composure, when he really wanted to jump the table and strangle the man.

"She had no desire to see him. I simply encouraged her not to upset herself and stay away from him." Finn shrugged.

"You mean you told her it wasn't good for your image that her father was on the streets." It was a statement more than a question and Finn didn't reply. He simply averted his eyes to the photographs of Darla.

They sat in silence for a few moments until Finn showed his impatience. "Get on with it. Who is that— who you claim to be my lover?" His voice held excessive exasperation.

"Darla Johnson." Dawson let the words sink in. To Finn's credit, Dawson never saw him flinch or react in any way.

"How would I know her again?"

"I understand she was your lover," Dawson reiterated.

"Who do you understand this from?" Finn was dancing around the truth, and Dawson knew it was just a matter of time before he'd say something he couldn't twist in another direction.

Dawson ignored the question. "When was the last time you saw her?"

"I don't know her." Finn was adamant, but his stance was shaken. His upper lip was suddenly beaded with sweat.

"She was a real estate agent. Maybe she handled

some of your deals." Dawson kept his face neutral of any emotion.

"Well, was she my real estate agent, or my lover?" Finn's voice was laced with sarcasm.

"You tell me." Dawson locked eyes with Finn. Neither of them would give in and the tension was palpable in the silence. Dawson held the stare, but continued. "I know you saw her on Tuesday night, and that you were the last one to see her."

Finn's composure slipped a notch. His face paled to a grayish-white, and he looked like he was about to collapse. "Yes, I saw her. And yes, we were having an affair." His tone lacked remorse. "Katie doesn't know, and I can't have that information out. It would hurt my reputation."

Dawson stood and walked over to the wall near the door, then leaned against it. "You realize my job isn't to protect your reputation. My job is stop a killer. Now, why don't we start once more at the beginning, and how about the truth this time?"

Finn's shoulders slumped in defeat. He rubbed his jaw before dropping his hands to his lap. "Darla and I had been seeing each other for a few months. She approached me about working on some of my real estate deals and things just progressed from there."

Dawson sat back down at the table. "And you saw her on Tuesday?"

"Yes. I went to her house. I told her she could continue to work on the property deals with me, but I was breaking it off with her. She wasn't happy."

"So, you weren't upset at all, just her?"

Finn sighed. "I was upset that she was screaming and yelling, carrying on over nothing. She'd made it known that I wasn't the first lover she'd taken. I didn't want to be involved. Besides, I love my wife."

"Love your wife? Yes, I can see that." Dawson cringed

at his own slip. He let emotions get in the way of his job, even if it was a harmless comment.

"You have no right to judge me!" Finn snapped.

"I'm not judging you. But I'd like to hear the truth without these nonsensical statements about the love you have for your wife, when you're screwing around on her."

"I saw Darla that night, and then I went home. She was in her house alone when I left. That's all there is." Finn's demeanor changed to irritation, and he was having a hard time concealing his anger.

"I'll be back. Stay here." Dawson grabbed the photos, sliding them into the folder before heading out the door. As he stepped into the bullpen, he noticed Captain Collins leaning against his desk, obviously waiting for him.

"You better have a good reason for hauling in Mr. O'Shannahan," Collins grumbled. "He'll call for your job, and I don't want the extra paperwork right now."

"Captain, he has a link to both murders. I couldn't not question him just because of his position." Dawson was not in the mood to try and pacify the local department. Sure, he had to work with them, but he didn't have to answer to the captain. He had his own chain of command to worry about. He was sick of people thinking that because of their job they could pull rank and circle around the law.

"I'm not disagreeing with you. Just be sure you have something before it goes too far." Captain pointed to the folder. "What do you have?"

"First vic was his father-in-law, second one was his lover that he says he was breaking off with the night of her death. Is that enough for questioning?"

"Don't get snarky with me, Dawson. I'm not going to tell you how to do your job, but I will make sure you don't bring down my precinct while doing it. That means, keep me in the loop and be certain you have what you need before hauling in anyone that could be a pain in my ass." He gestured toward the interrogation room where Finn sat.

Dawson nodded. "Understood."

Collins stood, and with a brief nod at Dawson, he made his way back to his office.

Dawson exhaled his frustration and threw the folder on his desk. He had nothing to hold Finn on other than a hunch and the word of an ex-con. He needed something that definitely tied him to the two victims, other than the obvious.

"Tough day?" Dawson turned at the sound of Ali's voice. She had a way of sending him off balance as soon as she spoke or whenever he looked at her. How long could he fight this attraction?

"I need a break in this case. Thought I had one, but I can't tie these ends together."

"Katie's set with the graveside service I've set up. She'll be there."

Dawson nodded. "I need to talk to her about her husband. He states she wanted nothing to do with her father. I didn't get that impression from her earlier."

"I agree. That doesn't sound right from the conversation I had with her."

"Hubby dearest was involved with the second vic, too. What a tangled web…" Dawson trailed off into thought.

"She might not be so quiet if she knew that." Ali reached out and put her hand on his arm. "She's definitely more talkative today about her dad."

Dawson acknowledged her with a small smile. His voice left him as the heat radiating into his arm from her touch had all his attention. He covered her hand with his own. "I'll go talk to her. Her husband can sit and stew for a little while."

"I've got to get back to my office. I'll talk to you later." Ali seemed reluctant to withdraw her hand and hesitated a moment before turning and walking away. The loss of her warmth lately had been hitting Dawson hard, and he knew it wouldn't be long before something more developed.

With a sigh, he headed to the break room where Katie was waiting. Upon entering the room, he took in the scene. She sat quietly at a round table, flipping through a magazine. Her posture was relaxed, and he couldn't help but mentally thank Ali for that.

"Can we talk for a minute?" He sat down at the table with her.

"Of course. What's going on that Finn is being held for?" Katie was matter of fact with no signs of being upset about the fact that her husband had been left in a room to wait out more questioning.

"Katie, let's go into the other room, so we'll have a little more privacy." Dawson stood and gestured toward a door off the break room that led to a small conference room. He walked slightly behind her with his hand on her back, gently guiding her, before shutting the door.

As soon as it clicked shut, Katie turned and faced him. "Was Finn involved in my father's death?"

"I don't know. He had ties to both of the victims." Dawson pulled out a chair for her to sit in.

"*Both* victims? There was another one?" Katie's voice was small and laced with fear.

"Yes, unfortunately."

"Who was the other one?" She straightened in the chair, putting up a brave front.

He hesitated. "Did you know a Darla Johnson?"

Katie shook her head. "Who was she?"

"She was a real estate agent who apparently was doing some business with your husband, and…"

"And?" Katie prompted.

"And they were involved, it looks like, *romantically*."

Katie offered a small smile. "Detective, please don't

try to be gentle with this. I knew my husband was screwing someone. I didn't know her name, but she's not the first, and I'm sure she won't be the last."

He sat back, relief easing the tension from his muscles. This woman was stronger than she appeared. She might be afraid of her husband, but she had an inner strength that would serve her well going forward.

"Why stay with him then?" He couldn't stop himself from asking.

"As you well know, it's all about appearances with Finn. He wouldn't tolerate a wife soiling his reputation."

"Has he hurt you?"

She smiled. "You're kind, detective, but we both know I'm not going to answer that."

He shook his head. He had a nagging feeling that Katie, in her own way, had in fact just answered the question, but he knew he couldn't say another word at that point. "Was Finn home on Tuesday?"

"I guess I'm supposed to say he was, but no he wasn't. He left the house right after dinner and didn't return home until well past eleven. I pretended to be asleep so he wouldn't know I knew what time he got home. The next morning, he mentioned I must have gone to bed early, because when he got home I was asleep. I never corrected him, but I'm not sure I can believe he was involved in these deaths." It was the most Dawson had ever heard her speak, and he watched her carefully as she did. It didn't appear rehearsed, but something didn't ring true either.

"Katie, I don't know he was involved, but something isn't adding up, and he knew both victims. Is there anything else you can tell me? Does he have tools or a workshop that he keeps?"

"Not that I'm aware, *per se*. He has some tools in the basement, but he doesn't ever go down there. The tools were ones that he states his father gave to him. He's not really the *get your hands* dirty type of man."

Dawson nodded. "I'm going to leave you in here so you can have a bit more privacy. I'll be back in a little bit."

She gestured to her cell phone. "Do you mind if I just make a phone call?"

"Go ahead. You're really here merely to wait for your husband, not to be questioned yourself."

Dawson exited the room. Katie didn't seem to give the impression that she cared much whether or not Finn was having an affair. Dawson couldn't help but wonder who she would be calling. Were there more secrets there than he realized?

thirteen

Dawson entered his house and threw his keys on the table. The day had proven to be nothing but frustrating. Questions weren't answered and he was no closer to finding the answers than before.

He changed into shorts and a t-shirt and headed to the garage, where he worked out his stress on his punching bag until he was drenched in sweat. Although the workout felt good, he hadn't alleviated the strain that this case was causing.

A knock on the porch door brought him back from his thoughts. He grabbed a towel and headed to answer it. When he opened the door, he came face to face with Ali. "Hey." He stepped back, allowing her entry.

"I just wanted to check on you. I know it was a tough day."

He flipped the towel to hang it around his neck, holding the ends of it to keep his hands occupied. Ali had changed into jeans that hugged her hips and a figure-clinging shirt. The V-neck dipped just low enough to give a hint of her cleavage—a tease that forced him to keep his eyes up on her face. Her smile made him realize she was waiting for a response.

He couldn't help but break out in a grin. "Yeah, frustrating day." He took a step closer to her, bringing them within kissing distance.

She stood there, watching him. Her breathing deepened, and he knew she was feeling the electricity between them. He stepped forward again, backing her up against the wall.

His hands slid from the towel and came to rest on her hips. Her breath hitched and he struggled to maintain the mere distance between them. He locked eyes with her, and his body stilled as her hands raised to grab the ends of the towel around his neck. Her tongue ran along her bottom lip as she slowly pulled him closer with the towel until their lips were teasing each other.

She sighed softly, and he pushed against her, the wall holding her captive between it and him. The kiss deepened until he pulled back suddenly, breathing heavily. Desire shined through her eyes as she looked at him, waiting.

"We can't." Dawson moved a fraction back, but they continued to have body on body contact.

Ali chuckled. "We can, but we won't."

"Technicality." He moved away reluctantly, relieved that she was being so understanding. "Can I get you a drink?"

"Got any beer?"

"You're speaking my language." He turned and headed to the kitchen. "Come on in."

He handed Ali a beer and gestured to the living room. As they settled in, he waited for her to say something.

"Well, I didn't come over here just to see you hot and sweaty." She grinned at him. "I came across some info that I thought might be useful."

He shook his head at her comment. He was playing with fire, and if he wasn't careful, he'd be the one who got burnt. "What info?" He was glad for the distraction.

"I was doing a little research on what kind of weapon leaves the wounds our victims had." She took another drink.

"And...you're killing me with suspense here," he prompted.

"Well, there is one alleged killer who has killed before with this style. We're talking about a hundred years ago, but I'm wondering if there's a connection. Have you heard of Lizzie Borden?"

Dawson sat forward. "*Lizzie Borden took an ax, and gave her mother forty whacks; when she saw what she had done, she gave her father forty-one.* That one?"

"Yes, although it wasn't forty whacks. The rhyme was a bit exaggerated."

"And you think the killings are similar? We obviously aren't dealing with the same person." His dry humor brought a laugh from Ali.

"Obviously. But we are looking at similarities. Same type of weapon. Lizzie destroyed her father's face much like these victims."

"Do you think we have a copycat here? Would a male imitate the infamous Lizzie?"

Ali shrugged. "Are you certain it is a male?"

"I'm pretty sure with the intensity that the blows seem to have. How many females could use that kind of power in a swing?"

"I don't know. I do know an adrenaline rush can be a powerful thing. But until we can tie up some of these loose ends, we won't know."

He nodded. "I just hope we don't end up with another dead body before we can do that."

Ali sat there sipping her beer, watching Dawson. She could hear his words, and she knew the information regarding Lizzie Borden could have waited until morning, but she had to admit seeing him hot and sweaty, and feeling his body pressed to hers, was well worth the trip. His simple words of we can't had been like a hit of icy cold water. Yet, she knew he felt it, too.

All she could think about was tasting those lips again, and feeling his body against hers.

She bit her lip to stop a soft moan from escaping and tried to focus on his words...don't end up with another dead body...

Right. It was the case they needed to think about.

fourteen

Dawson changed into black jeans and a black hooded sweatshirt. His gun, holstered against his left ribs, brought a sense of comfort. Guilt washed over him for sending Ali home so he could do his nightly routine. She knew what he was doing, and yet didn't say a word to discourage him. He got the impression she wanted him to ask her to help, but he just wasn't at that point yet. He couldn't allow anyone into this aspect of his life.

Inhaling deeply, he turned toward the door, drew his hood up over his head and walked out into the night. It was already 10:00 p.m., an hour later than when he usually made this trip. It used to be nightly, but lately, he'd cut it back to every two-to-three nights. The heartache it caused was like an addiction. It pulled him back time and time again. He couldn't give up hope. Not yet.

He turned down into the first alley off Sixth Street. The stale scent of urine and feces hit him. He took shallow breaths to control how much of it he would smell. The farther into the alley he went, the stronger the odor became, mixed with rotting food from the overflowing dumpsters.

Hesitating for a moment, he closed his eyes, trying to will away the mental picture of Sara living like this. He pulled his strength from the bond they always held between them and continued forward. The faint flame from a fire in a trash can at the far end of the dead-end alley caught his eye. It was the place where most of the occupants of surrounding alleys would hole up on cold evenings to try and stay warm.

Dawson admired the homeless' instincts for survival. And they were survivors, no matter what life had dealt them; they were still breathing day after day. He knew only too well how an empty soul continued to move through the moments. He wished he'd grabbed his black baseball cap to hide his eyes, but it was too late now. He pulled the hood of the sweatshirt as far as he could over his eyes and headed toward the trash can where surprisingly there were only five occupants hanging around. He smiled when he recognized Hannah right away.

She glanced up at him as he came to stand next to her. The warmth emanating from the fire was a relief, reminding him of just how cool the night air had become.

"I know you?" Hannah spoke quietly.

"Yes, ma'am."

"Ahhh, that young detective. Why are you here? These folks won't take kindly to you showing up."

Dawson took a step closer to the fire, allowing the heat to warm his hands. "I wanted you to know that Eugene's service will be at the cemetery two days from now at noon. I thought you would know who'd want to attend."

"Why would any of us go?"

"You knew him and protected his things when he was killed. That's friendship, and he should have friends there to say goodbye to him."

Hannah just nodded as she stole another glance at him. "That it?"

"No. I figure you know just about everyone out here. I'm looking for Sara."

"I don't know no Sara."

His stance stiffened. "Please, Hannah. If you do know her, tell her I'm looking for her. She has a place with me to come home to."

"What's she to you?" Hannah reached for his elbow and drew him away from the fire, into the shadows.

"My sister."

"Don't know her."

Frustration ripped through Dawson. He wanted to scream and release the tension that had built up for years. Damn Sara for doing this to him. He was not their parents, and she knew it. He had no idea why she'd continue this torturous route.

"Thanks, ma'am. Remember what I said if you come across her." He reached for her hand. "Let others know about Eugene's service. He deserves a proper goodbye."

He faded into the shadows and started back out the alley, staying close to the wall. His eyes had adjusted to the dimness, but the shadows darkened the world around him, and for a brief moment, he realized how good it felt to slip into the unknown.

He went through the motions of checking another four or five alleys, asking people here and there if they knew Sara. Always the same answer—no. He lost count before he decided to call it a night.

Disappointment didn't seem to exist anymore from these searches; instead he expected no results, yet he couldn't stop searching. In the depth of his heart, he knew Sara was still out there.

His thoughts turned to the memories he had with her. The time he covered for her when she'd slipped away for a party one night after being forbidden to go. Big brother to the rescue. He'd covered for her a lot. Her only rebellion against the rules was to go out at night. They'd lived in such a strict household, his parents operating out of fear. Instead of protecting their kids, his parents ended up losing everyone in their life—but him, out of loyalty only—because of their attitude and short leash.

He stopped abruptly on the steps to the porch when he saw the piece of paper stuck between the door and the jamb. He pulled it out and looked around for some sort of sign that someone had been there. Nothing.

Stop searching. I'm fine. S.

He clenched the paper in his fist. Sara would do this every so often, and he was furious with her for not showing herself. His instinct was to crumble the paper and throw it aside. Instead, he drew in a deep breath and went into his house.

He opened the side drawer of the table near the door. Inside was every note Sara had left him. All saying the same thing. He jotted down the date on the back of this one, just like the others. The only thing consistent was that the notes appeared every three months, almost to the day. He slid the new note into the drawer and closed it. She'd made it through another three months, and he took solace in that fact, even as the pain tore through his heart. For whatever reason, she would not give him more than this.

Morning brought a sunless day. Gray clouds hung low over the city and they matched Dawson's mood. Lack of sleep and frustration were not a good combination, and he decided it was best not to go into the station first thing this morning. He sent a brief text to Brown letting him know he was following up on some leads, and he was to let him know ASAP of any developments. The text back was simply Read the paper.

Dawson frowned at the text. He was working outside of the office, not sitting around enjoying coffee and a paper. Another text popped up on his phone, this time from Ali. *Did you see the paper?* He'd already left the house and hadn't looked at his newspaper this morning. He headed for the nearest newsstand and picked up another copy.

O'SHANNAHAN BROUGHT IN FOR
QUESTIONING ON MURDERS.

The headline screamed at him. Not good. Dawson was surprised he hadn't heard from the captain yet. He scanned the article. An anonymous tip had brought the news to the reporter's attention. A picture of O'Shannahan and Katie leaving the police station was centered on the front page.

Only the people in the station had known Finn was there that day. A leak in the department? Dawson shook his head. His temples throbbed as a headache started. He turned toward the station. There'd be no avoiding this confrontation with the captain. Another text came through from Ali. *Well?*

Just saw it. Will talk later.

He parked his car in front of the station and looked up at the gray building. He'd always enjoyed the architecture of it and thought of it as a safe refuge from the daily grind. Yet, today with the dark clouds overhead, the grayness of the building was magnified and intimidating. It was very similar to the State Police offices, which he called home, but lately, he worked with local precincts more and more.

His walk up on the granite steps was slow and deliberate. He dreaded this meeting. In his mind, he went through every person in the station that he had seen that day. Not one could he pinpoint as someone who would leak information of a suspect. Minutes blurred as he moved in what seemed to be slow motion through the door, down the hall to the front of the captain's office. The door was half open.

He pushed it fully open and found the captain sitting behind his desk. The man nodded to him. Silence was deafening as Dawson took a seat across from the desk, waiting for the captain to start talking. He watched the captain's expression, neutral and unyielding of any clue as to the path this conversation would take.

Dawson cleared his throat. "You saw the paper, I take it."

The captain sat back in his chair, tips of his fingers pressed together at his mouth, but still silent. A small smile played at the captain's lips as Dawson waited for some sort of a reply. "Not sure which words weren't understood when I said not to cause me extra paperwork."

Dawson fought to keep a straight face. "I think I know who it was."

"Way ahead of you. I made a phone call this morning. I have contacts everywhere. You know that. Damage control is already done."

"And?"

"You're right in your thought process. I'm sure you have work to do instead of sitting here." Captain picked up a pen and went back to the papers in front of him. Dismissal obvious.

Dawson made his way to his desk. "Brown, where are we on this?"

"Still no weapon."

"Do some research on Lizzie Borden for me, please. It may be the same MO."

"Sir?" His confusion came out through the single word.

Dawson looked up, shaking his head before speaking. "Obviously, we know it's not her, Brown. She died in the early 1900s. But I want the info anyway." Dawson picked up the newspaper on his desk. "By the way, I'll be attending Eugene Henry's memorial service tomorrow. I want to see who shows up."

"Should I be there?" Brown asked.

"Meet me in the morning about eleven outside the cemetery gates. We'll set up a plan then."

Dawson grabbed his phone. *Time to talk?* He punched in a text to Ali.

A reply text immediately beeped in. *Come to my office.*

Dawson headed for the door. *Why* was the only thing that rang through his mind. Why and how. And yet, who never was a question. The leaked information about O'Shannahan wasn't really as much as a surprise as it should have been, but he wondered Ali's thoughts on it.

He stepped into Ali's office to find her sitting at her desk, partially concealed by a stack of files and medical books. "Are you here?"

"Half crushed by all this stuff." She stood and smiled at him. "So?"

He moved the stack of files to the floor so he could have a good view of Ali as they talked. He couldn't help but admire how simply beautiful she looked with her hair pulled back in a ponytail and no makeup. His heart gave an extra beat as he watched her. Realizing she was waiting for him to say something, he cleared his throat and could feel his face redden.

"Captain did damage control already. I don't know why she did it, unless it's just an opportune time for her to get some revenge on him."

Ali cocked her head at him. "*Her?*"

"I think it was Katie who leaked the story. She asked me if she could make a phone call. Who else? No one in the department would have leaked that information."

Ali smirked. "Interesting. She's got more backbone than I pegged her for."

"I had that same thought the other day."

"Great minds and all that, huh?" She winked at him.

He gestured to the folders. "I'll let you get back to work, and I've got some things to follow up on. Talk later?"

She nodded and he started for the door without another word. He stopped and glanced back to see her pull the stack of files up from the floor to hide behind them once more.

fifteen

Dawson stood at the sink, sipping his coffee and looking out his back window. Unwelcome rain poured down. The day was fitting for a funeral, to say the least. The clouds were darker than yesterday, and today the heavens had opened. Not the best for a graveside service.

He had a feeling O'Shannahan wouldn't show up with his wife for his father-in-law's service, but he wasn't convinced how involved Finn was in the murders. He wasn't the type of man to get actual blood on his hands; he was the hiring-out type.

Dawson arrived at the cemetery at quarter of eleven. The black, wrought-iron fence around the perimeter looked even more sinister on this dark day. He drove into the cemetery, maneuvering the car around the winding roads, searching the area near the grave. A tent had been set up over the dug plot, extending out a few feet on both sides. At least people would be out of the rain for a few moments.

He parked several rows over from the area. Looking around, he had a clear view of the main entrance. The side entrance was the only other access opened that day.

The others were blocked off as was the routine for graveside services. As he drove back around to the outside of the cemetery, he saw Brown waiting for him.

"I want you at the side entrance." Dawson spoke without preamble. "Keep an eye out for anyone coming in who you don't think should be here."

"Who are we looking for?" Brown asked.

"Not sure, but I wonder if our killer will show up."

Brown nodded and drove off to his post. Dawson turned around and saw Katie driving into the cemetery. She was alone. No surprise there that her husband wouldn't show. Dawson followed her until she parked. She stayed in the car until he approached her window, then stepped out and opened her umbrella.

"Finn not with you?" Dawson asked.

"You knew he wouldn't be here. He's trying to stay out of the public eye at the moment."

He took her elbow and started toward the tent set up by the grave. "I think we both know why that is. Want to tell me why you did it?"

She glanced at him. "Did what?"

"Now's not the time to be coy. How about some honesty?"

"We'll have to talk after the service. I don't want to do this now." She pulled her arm away from him. "Later."

He watched as she walked the last few steps to the tent. Turning away, he headed for a large tree that was a few rows over and found a spot to watch from. As people started entering the cemetery, he kept his eyes open for anything…anything that would help him break this case. Instead of answers, he was running into more questions. Nothing added up.

He couldn't help but let his mind wander to an earlier time, a sunny day where love reflected from the love they were burying. His grandmother had been a strong influence in his life. A woman who'd kept him sane when Sara had run away. The day she'd died, and subsequently the day they'd buried her, he could never forget the way the sun hit his face as the tears had rolled down his cheeks. The warmth was a gentle reminder of the love from his grandmother that would always be with him.

Dawson—chilled to the bone—stood stiff, watching the service go on. The cold had seeped through and cleared his mind of the happier memories. Hannah and a handful of other homeless people had arrived. A few of Katie's friends who knew her father showed up. No one out of the ordinary, and the fact that Finn was not there, was glaringly obvious. Katie handled herself with dignity and quietly thanked each person for being there.

When the service was over, Dawson watched Katie head to her car. She hesitated briefly before getting in and driving away. The rain had let up, but the gray skies kept his mood somber. He glanced toward the grave one more time before turning to his vehicle. On the windshield, under one of the wipers, was a manila envelope.

Dawson squeezed his arm into his rib to feel the reassuring bulge of his gun holstered to his side. He glanced around. There was no one left at the cemetery, and he hadn't seen anyone near his car. He pulled out his phone and called Brown.

"Are you still at the side gate?"

"Yes, sir, but everyone is gone now."

"Found an envelope on my car, but I have no idea who put it there." Dawson continued scanning the surrounding area. "Go ahead and get out of here. Did you finish getting that stuff on Lizzie Borden together?"

"Just about. I'll have it to you tomorrow."

"Thanks." Dawson ended the call without another word.

All he wanted was a cup of hot coffee and a place to thaw. He pulled out his phone again and sent a text to Ali: *meet me at the diner at the corner of 5th and Main. Ten minutes.*

He didn't wait for a reply before driving off. The diner. Not that the coffee was spectacular, but there was something about the place that called to him.

When he arrived, he headed straight to the booth in the corner. Sitting with his back to the wall, facing the door, he surveyed the room. It was pretty empty with the exception of a few people sitting at the counter. He searched for Beth, assuming she'd be the only waitress on duty again. And sure enough, she came out of the kitchen and scowled when she saw him. Always a good impression he made on people.

Beth brought over a coffee mug and filled it. "Anything else?"

"Hi Beth. Amy back yet?"

"Do you see her?" Beth said sarcastically and walked away.

Her sardonic behavior surprised him, and once again, she hadn't made direct eye contact. He couldn't help but smile as he remembered Ali giving him a hard time for baiting Beth.

He sipped his coffee, keeping both hands wrapped around the mug. The heat soon penetrated through his frozen fingers and he relaxed a bit. He looked at the envelope lying in front of him on the laminate table. He hadn't waited long before Ali entered the diner. He caught her eyes and raised a hand to get her attention.

He sat quietly as she took her seat, while looking at the table. She nodded at the envelope. "What's this?"

He hadn't opened it yet. "It was left on my car at the cemetery." He tapped his fingers on the folder.

"Well, open it. What are you waiting for?"

He snickered. "I was waiting until my hands thawed so I could move my fingers."

The folder had no writing on the outside. He opened it and pulled out a single sheet of paper. On it were three addresses. One was not far from there, another on the other side of the city, and the third was, ironically, the diner. There was nothing else in the folder that would indicate who'd dropped it off.

"What now?" Ali broke his concentration.

"There has to be a connection." He took another sip of his coffee. The addresses were typed out.

Ali gestured for Beth, and surprisingly, she came right over. "Coffee, please, Beth." Ali made eye contact and gave her a smile.

Beth nodded before whisking away to get the coffee pot. She returned momentarily, and addressed Ali directly, "anything else?"

"No, thank you. This will be good for now." Ali waited until Beth walked away before turning her attention back to Dawson. "What now?"

"Guess I need to see what I can find out about these other two addresses."

"Nothing jumps out at you for any connection?"

He frowned. "Nothing, and yet that doesn't surprise me. I just wonder who put it on my car. It wasn't like there were a lot of people at the cemetery."

"Okay. I'll talk to you later. I've got some emails to answer, and I think I'll do it here while I have another cup of coffee."

He nodded as he threw down a few dollars on the table and made his way to the door. Saturday afternoon and he was headed for the office for what probably would be a long night doing some research.

sixteen

I stroked the blade of the hatchet. I had laid low, but the itch to continue with my list was one I couldn't scratch without the excitement of the kill. The list had three names left on it. The last two were the crux of my actions. They would pay, and very soon.

I drew on the cloak and covered my head with its hood as I stood next to the table. Unrecognizable and able to fit right into the shadows. The blackness of the cloak had been the perfect choice when I'd put this plan into motion. Midnight black. What a perfect time and color for my adventure. The black gloves comforted me as the supple leather soothed my skin with each movement. I lifted the hatchet from the table, feeling the weight of it in my hand, fueling my desire to use it...to take life and gain control.

I stepped out of the room and moved stealthily down the hallway, staying close to the wall. The hallway was lit every so often with only a small sconce light, casting shadows on the floor and walls. If I didn't know better, I would think spirits moved within this hallway. Spirits that could tell secrets of lives past.

Stopping just inside the exit to the world, I closed my

eyes and envisioned my next victim. I inhaled deeply and exhaled in a timed, controlled pace, then stepped from the building into the shadows of the night. The rain was in my favor with no moon to give any extra light. The city had gone downhill in many ways over the years, but significant for me was the fact that street lights were no longer repaired, adding darkness to my cover.

I turned up the first alley I came to, took a sharp right, and followed it back as it mazed through the south side of the city. This was one of the few alleys that didn't dead end and I knew it like the back of my hand. I'd spent years wandering these corridors, trying to figure out routes for this very moment. My attack route, my exit route. I ran through them over and over in my mind. There was only one goal for the evening and that was to quiet the voices screaming at me to get on with it.

I came to the alley where I'd done my first killing. I still tingled with the thought of it and could feel the warm blood squirting up and hitting my face. The power in my hand wielding the hatchet, taking control with every swing. The second kill had brought on the same reaction, fueling a fire within me that couldn't be extinguished now. I wondered if I'd be able to squelch it once I finished the list.

I stopped a couple of yards from the main road. My eyes trained on the road, ears listening for any sound around me. The night was silent. I crept forward, staying to the wall of the building at the corner, shielding me from any light that might come through the thick clouds. A smile tugged at the corners of my mouth as anticipation built inside of me. I heard the sound of the blood rushing as my pulse quickened and my adrenaline soared.

No cars approached from either direction. The corner streetlight was out. I darted across the road into the alley. Leaning against the brick wall in the darkness, I took a deep breath. I'd never been so daring to cross a main street before, never had been bold enough to leave an alleyway. The sense of accomplishment at not being seen filled me with confidence. I crept along a wall that came behind the corner diner that the detective had recently become so fond of.

The owner was ritualistic and never wavered from his routine. The church clock rang its gong. One, two, three…I counted until it hit eleven. My golden number. The back door from the diner swung open and out stepped Charlie, the owner. He perched on a stack of crates and lit up a cigarette. I watched him with amusement as he smoked. The last cigarette he would ever smoke. I allowed him that final luxury.

I stepped out of the shadows, my right hand gripping the handle of my weapon under my cloak. I was to the side of him and he didn't see me for a few seconds. "Hey, what are you doing out here?"

He stood to confront me, and I pushed the hood off my head.

"*You.*"

The one word registered with me, and I jerked the hatchet up, hitting him square in the chin with the butt of it. He fell backward to the ground, dazed. I stood over him, grinned, and swung down. The blade hit his nose with a sickening crunch.

In quick passes, I raised my arm and came down hard, harder with each stroke. Blood sprayed up and its warmth on my skin fueled me. He lay still beneath me after eleven hits that crisscrossed over each other, giving no real indication of what his face had looked like. I wiped the blade across his shirt to get the bulk of the blood from it.

Looking down at him, I felt a weight lift off my shoulders. Control was back in my hands.

I took one further look at the blood pooling on the ground beneath his head, and I smiled. The stories our spirits could tell. The thought played through my mind as I turned and left the scene. One more name to cross off the list. One step closer to the final goal.

Fading into the shadows, I returned to the spot where I'd begun the evening. My steps were light and my mood even lighter as I followed the maze back.

seventeen

Another one. Behind the diner.

Dawson looked at his phone and the incoming text from Officer Brown. His stomach clenched at those words. *Another one.* He was no closer to finding out who'd done the first two, and now it appeared by all definitions he was dealing with a serial killer.

He punched in a response to Brown, *on my way*, and headed to the door. He hadn't slept much last night. After spending hours combing the streets looking for Sara, he'd finally returned home to just toss and turn all night. He was seeing Sara in his dreams, blood coming from her face sometimes, and occasionally with her features completely unrecognizable. His nerves were already frayed from the nightmare, and now, another victim compounded them.

With coffee in hand, he'd been on the way to the station early. So much for getting a jump on the day. He moved his head from side to side, trying to work out the tension. This case was taking its toll and there didn't seem to be an end in sight. He felt like he was drowning already, and yet waves just kept pounding over him.

He headed for the diner. There had to be a connection beyond O'Shannahan. It just didn't sit right in his gut that the politician was behind the first two killings, despite his connection to both victims.

Dawson pulled up behind the medical examiner's van. He walked out behind the diner and found Ali kneeling beside the victim.

"What do we have?" Dawson asked as he knelt as well.

Ali glanced at him. "More of the same. I'd say time of death close to midnight."

"And no one saw anything?" He looked around for Brown.

"Nope." Ali snapped off her gloves. "Apparently, the waitress found him."

Dawson took in the scene as he stood. Blood congealed beneath the victim's head. Never any footprints in the blood. Frustration washed over him. "Where's Brown?"

"Inside, I think."

Dawson turned and went through the back door into the kitchen. The stale smell of grease and cigarette smoke assaulted him. He peered around the kitchen, noticing a knife on the cutting board, along with bacon strips that had been cut. Flies hovered over the meat. He swallowed hard. After seeing this kitchen, he probably wouldn't be eating here again.

He moved around the chef's counter and headed into the seating area. Brown was at the counter talking with the waitress, Beth. Dawson looked about. The room was empty, except for those two. He moved closer and listened.

"What time did you get here?" Brown asked.

"I arrived at the same time I always do, six-thirty." Beth glanced over at Dawson. "Charlie always handled everything himself from ten at night until I got here early the next morning. It's not like it's busy that time anyway."

"And you found him right off?"

Beth shook her head. "No. I filled the sugar containers and ketchup bottles. Then I went into the kitchen and I didn't see him, but he goes out back a lot to smoke."

"How long were you out there before you found him?"

"I yelled for him a couple of times, and when he didn't answer, I went to the door." She shuddered. "And found him...like that."

Dawson nodded to Brown. "Beth, was anyone else here when you arrived?"

"No. It was empty like usual."

Brown reached out and handed her his card. "If you think of anything, please call me."

"So, I'm free to go?"

"For now. We may have more questions." Dawson wandered around the diner as Brown finished up with Beth. The floor hadn't been mopped and the tables weren't wiped down.

"Well, what I am supposed to do now?" Beth's voice broke through Dawson's thoughts.

"What do you mean?"

"I assume you're closing the place. That means I'm out of work."

He turned and stared at her. "Well, as you know the owner has been killed. We need to close the diner because it's a crime scene."

"Who's going to pay me so I can pay my bills?"

"I guess you'll have to see what happens to the diner. Did Charlie have any other family besides you?"

Beth glared at him. "No."

Dawson saw the flash of anger in her eyes, and it hit him that this was the first time she'd ever made direct eye contact. The mousy persona was back as quickly as it had disappeared, leaving Beth's face expressionless and her eyes downcast.

"We'll let you know when we're done," he said to her, "and you can come back in to clean."

She grabbed her purse and stormed to the door, glancing back over her shoulder at him before leaving. He waited until she was gone before he addressed the young officer. "Lock that door, Brown."

"Yes, sir."

Dawson sighed. Seems he'd never break him of saying sir, though if the truth be known, he respected Brown for the very thing that irritated him.

Dawson looked around the diner one more time before heading for the back door. He stopped briefly in the kitchen, surveying the surroundings again: Food on the counters covered in flies, and dirty dishes stacked in the sink. There was no sign of struggle. It hadn't started in there, which meant the victim must have been out on a smoke break when the attack happened.

He continued out through the door, squinting as he looked around the alley. The dumpster was overflowing. Stacked-up crates made a place to sit, and with the amount of cigarette butts on the ground surrounding them, it must have been the spot where Charlie sat and smoked.

Dawson glanced over his shoulder to the door of the diner. It was only a few feet away. Out of all the crime scenes, this one was probably the most visible...if an alley could be visible. But it was closest to the street—a dead end—that didn't allow for a lot of hiding. The perp must've come from the street.

His eyes rested on Ali as she gave orders for the body to be bagged and prepared for the trip to the morgue. Even in the worst of circumstances, she seemed to shine. She portrayed a confidence in her work that amazed him, given the brutality of what she saw on a regular basis. He cast a small smile as she looked over at him. Mentally shaking off the warmth only she could send him, he turned toward the dumpster. He looked at the ground around it. No footprints.

Frustration coursed through him at the lack of evidence at all of these crime scenes. How could this killer possibly not leave footprints of any kind?

He chuckled to himself. Maybe he was dealing with Lizzie Borden's ghost. It might be a fleeting thought, yet he couldn't help but wonder what caused Lizzie to kill her father and stepmother, and did it have a connection to these deaths?

"Hey, I'm headed back to the morgue." Ali's quiet voice brought Dawson around to find her right behind him. "You okay?"

"As okay as I can be with this mess. What am I missing?" He shook his head.

"I don't know. I haven't been much help, since I'm not finding much myself with the autopsies. But, Dawson, don't take this personally."

"How can I not take this personally? This killer is playing with me, always two steps ahead of me. And unless I get a jump on this perp, we're going to be looking at more dead bodies." He couldn't hide the irritation laced his voice.

She reached out and rested a hand on his arm. "What does your gut say?"

"There's a pattern I'm not seeing. There has to be." He gestured around him. "But what is it? Besides the fact that I'm clueless."

"Well, that's a male thing, but that's a different type of clueless." She slowly drew her hand away from his arm. "You'll figure it out. What is it you tell Brown? Think outside the box?"

Dawson nodded. "I'll text you later." He didn't wait for her to respond, but turned and went back inside the diner. There had to be a clue there, he knew it somehow. This was the center spot for all the killings. They were all tied here somehow, but how? He wasn't sure yet, but it was time to step out of the box and really look at his surroundings.

eighteen

I wandered onto the bridge leading to the other side of the tracks—the side where the inhabitants were strangers to the rest of the city. It was an invisible line that spoke volumes about both sides. Standing on the middle of the bridge, I looked over the river as it twisted and turned down stream. The city lights weren't as bright as they used to be, but somehow, they still outshined the other side that had a perpetual shadow cast over it.

With a sigh, I turned and finished crossing the bridge. The silence was deafening as I moved toward the sidewalk that ran the length of Highland Road. I'd walked this path daily for as long as I could remember. The houses lining the street had seen better days. That side of the city held no promise or hope to the people that lived—if you could call it living—there.

I stopped short in front of Highland Road and faced the large sprawling Victorian. The paint was chipped and one couldn't tell any longer what color it had been in the past. The black shutters hanging by a single screw gave the house a look of being possessed.

Not a light was on inside, nor even the outside light for that matter. It might as well be abandoned for the way it looked to passersby. I pushed open the wrought-iron gate at the end of the cement walk leading to the front porch. The groan of metal grated my nerves as I moved through and continued up the blocks lining the way. Grass tufts poked through them, growing out of control from lack of attention. I picked my way carefully along, knowing all too well the areas where the blocks had been heaved up by the sand shifting underneath them.

I ascended the steps, one at a time, until I stood facing the front door. As I turned the handle to open it, I couldn't help but cringe as I stepped through the doorway. I hated this house with a passion. It was evil through and through.

The house was quiet, except for the scurrying of footsteps through the ceiling. I almost smiled at the thought of my only company being the rats in the walls. I wondered if they'd found their new toy yet. The sound of a heavy object falling upstairs alerted me to the fact the rats had probably started to overrun the attic. A smile curled up the corners of my mouth, and with a nod, I sat down in the living room.

The darkness consumed me, inside and out. I could sit for hours without light or noise around me. Depriving my senses of these things only heightened my awareness of my surroundings. I'd spent too long coming up with a plan. It was being executed now and there was no stopping the wrecking ball that had already started the damage.

nineteen

Dawson poured himself yet another cup of coffee. His stomach churned in protest at the liquid diet he'd kept all day. Between the coffee and the stress, he wouldn't be surprised if he ended up with an ulcer over this case. Mug in hand, he wandered back into the room that held the victimology board. Charlie's name was slated under the Victim #3 heading. Dawson stared at the board, willing the answers to jump out at him.

"I thought I'd find you here." Ali spoke as she placed a bag on the table behind him. "Bet you haven't eaten all day either."

He shook his head and turned to face her. "Any news regarding the vic today?"

"Nothing that we don't already know. Charlie Walker, owner of the diner. Facial mutilation just like the other vics, I'm guessing, from some sort of hand-held ax-type weapon."

Dawson slid into the hard, wooden chair. He nodded toward the bag. "What's that?"

"Dinner. I figured you'd be working late tonight with

this new killing, and you can't live on coffee." She pulled out two containers from the bag and passed one to him. "Mind if I join you? Maybe you can bounce some theories off me."

"Sure, if I had any." He opened the container and found a salad with steak tips on top and a side of warm pita bread. "Trying to kill me with this healthy stuff?"

She grinned. "You need to take better care of yourself."

He feigned disgust, but dug into the salad, realizing just how hungry he was. He was still shoveling in the food when Ali placed a bottle of water in front of him.

"I've got coffee," he mumbled.

"You'll dehydrate yourself with all that coffee. Drink the water."

"Jeez, you'd think you were a doctor or something." He rolled his eyes, but opened the bottle anyway.

"Yeah, or *something*." She pointed to the board as she slid into a chair across the table from him. "What's the connection between the three vics?" She talked as she opened her own salad, but he could see that instead of steak tips, it was topped with grilled chicken.

"Well, the first two had a connection to O'Shannahan, but number three didn't that I know of. The only link I can find is that the diner is center to them all. Eugene would go there in the morning every day, Darla frequented it, and of course, Charlie owned it."

"Okay. Do you know of any other patrons that had an issue with Charlie?"

Dawson shook his head. "I still haven't been able to locate the other waitress, Amy, who apparently stopped showing up for work about the time of the first incident. She seems to have fallen off the face of the earth. Not sure if there's a connection with that or not, but Brown and I both have canvassed her neighborhood, made phone calls…nothing."

"So, what's your theory?" Ali questioned.

"I'm chasing a ghost." He stood and studied the board. "What do you know about Lizzie Borden? From my understanding, she was acquitted for the crime, but no one else was ever arrested."

"There've always been a lot of rumors and speculation around the murders. I studied the transcripts of the trial online. It appeared that she was acquitted because she was a woman, and the judge didn't want to hang a woman." Ali pushed her now-empty container away from her.

"That's the theory behind her being acquitted? Because she was a woman?"

Ali cleaned up the empty containers. "There was also the speculation that Lizzie and her sister, Emma, were abused by their father, and Lizzie did it to stop the abuse. Of course, there was also speculation that Lizzie did it because she and her sister were to inherit a fortune."

"Any proof to those rumors?" He watched Ali, trying to keep his mind on what she was saying. The simple act of clearing remnants of dinner away had never looked so sexy, and holy shit, did Ali look sexy. His eyes strayed down her body as she moved to the trash can to get rid of the containers and slowly drifted back up before she turned to look at him.

"No proof to anything. There are such contradictory statements. The court transcripts indicated her answers weren't very in-depth or even coherent at times."

"How much have you looked into this?"

She shrugged. "I'm a medical examiner. Things like this fascinate me."

"Do you think there was any truth to the rumors of molestation?"

"To Lizzie?" Ali asked and shook her head. "No way of knowing."

He looked at the board again. "Okay, so if we go with

that theory, we possibly could be looking for someone who's been abused. That narrows it down."

"There has to be more of a connection between the three vics than just the diner."

Dawson paced the floor, back and forth, his head bent down as he focused on the floorboards he walked over. He clenched his hands and relaxed them repeatedly as he strode across the floor and back again.

"Wes." Ali spoke softly. He paused and looked at her. "Why don't we go for a walk outside? It might help clear your mind."

"I've got too much work to do." He pointed at the board.

"And pacing the floor in this room is not going to give you the answers you need. Come on." She threw the bag of trash she'd cleaned up in the waste can at the door.

He sighed, but followed her. "You know this isn't going to help."

"Have you *tried* walking to clear your thoughts?" She glanced back at him. "I know you haven't, so don't even attempt to convince me you have."

She linked her arm with his as they exited the station. He hadn't realized what time it was, but the sun was sitting low in the sky. There was a chill in the air, yet neither of them seemed bothered by it. "Okay, which way are we going?"

She turned and guided him with their linked arms to the right. They walked down the sidewalk in silence. He tried to look ahead, but kept catching glimpses of her looking around as they walked. "What are you searching for?"

"Clues." She smiled. "It's always been a relaxation method for me to walk around the city and take in what I normally wouldn't see. It clears the mind and opens it to possibilities of what could be, or what is right in front of you."

He shook his head. This woman was amazing. She seemed to know exactly what he needed to hear and see.

"What is it you were telling Brown with that first murder?" Ali broke into his thoughts. "Look at it, really see it."

"But we aren't in the middle of a crime scene here."

"This city became the crime scene as soon as this person killed the first innocent bystander. So, look around. What do you see?" They came to a stop and moved to the edge of the sidewalk.

He looked around. "Filth. When did this city get so run down?"

"That's superficial. Look deeper," she prodded.

He looked at *her*. The low setting sun made her hair shine and he had the urge to just bring her into his arms and kiss her. "I'd rather look at you."

She shook her head at him. "Seriously. Come on."

Reluctantly, he scanned across the street. Another alley. This city was full of them and most had become homes to the homeless. He, himself, had wandered these alleys looking for Sara. He and Ali were about a block from the station, headed toward the railroad tracks. He'd hoped he wouldn't have to go over there to search for Sara. That side of the city was evil. Evil. It was an area that had become abandoned except for the people who had lived there all their lives. No one new ever moved there because of its run-down state and the rumors that it was haunted.

Budget cuts had hit the city of Leighton hard and the police station was running on minimal personnel, hence why the state police were so quick to be called. To take on a serial killer without a lot of help was exhausting, and yet, to a killer would be beneficial.

"What are you thinking?" Ali asked, squeezing his arm.

"The other side of the tracks…gives me the creeps, and I've seen a lot of stuff."

She looked up at him, confusion on her face. "I guess my question is, if that's the worst side of the city, why are the crimes over here in an area that doesn't have the crime rate that the other section does?"

"Good question. Is it a statement on the part of the killer?"

She shrugged. "Could be. Does the killer come from that side of the tracks?"

He turned back toward the station. "Come on. This isn't helping."

"You are so stubborn. You aren't thinking outside the box." She stopped him.

"Outside or inside the box, there still aren't any answers." He glanced down at her. "Besides, it's time to call it a night. I need a couple hours of sleep before I jump into it tomorrow. I'm just too tired to look at all the angles right now."

Ali sighed.

He couldn't help but smile at her. "Even with your exasperation…" He paused as he rolled his eyes, "you have the cutest sighing skills."

She winked. "Apparently, my power to distract you works quite well."

He pulled her close, leaned down, and gently kissed her on the forehead. "You have no idea how distracting you are." Her arms slid around his waist, and he nearly groaned aloud as he felt himself harden at her touch.

He closed his eyes, willing himself to cool down. When he opened his eyes, she was looking up at him, smiling. She slowly ran her tongue over her lips. This time, he couldn't stifle the groan.

She giggled as she moved away. "Time for you to get home and get that much-needed sleep." She slipped her hand into his.

twenty

Although he craved sleep, Dawson couldn't bring himself to shut off the computer once he got home. He did search after search on Lizzie Borden and came up with the same information that Ali had shared with him. He read through the court transcripts and found nothing to give insight into whether she was guilty. There was nothing to indicate innocence either.

The only thing that stood out was the victims that he was investigating had only ten to twelve slashes to the face that could be counted. Apparently, Lizzie had done about nineteen whacks to her stepmother, and her father had ten or eleven. No similarity there, but the same type of weapon, or so Dawson assumed, since they hadn't found a weapon yet.

He glanced at the clock and groaned. It was already 4:00 a.m. There'd been no sleep for him. He'd take a shower and head for the station. His mind raced as he let the hot water rain over him. There had to be a connection somewhere.

What was he missing?

He moved through his shower and got dressed on autopilot.

He no sooner walked into the station when it hit him—the envelope, the addresses. The diner made no sense other than it was the third murder. Though the other two were not the locations of the other killings. He needed to check those addresses out, and hopefully, that would be the break he was looking for.

He pulled the addresses off the board and headed for the first one. 32 Chestnut Street. That was only three blocks over from the station. He sent a text to Brown letting him know where he was going and told him to meet him there.

Dawson strode down the sidewalk with purpose, praying that he'd find the break he needed. He didn't know where the file had come from, but he'd been too distracted by the third killing to look into the addresses yesterday.

He arrived at the location just as Brown stepped out of his car. Standing in front of the door, Dawson turned and looked around. It was a brick building with an alley on each side. Same type of old alley as found around the City—filthy and full of homeless people. He turned back to the building. Nothing stood out to him as out of the ordinary. He tried the door and it opened silently into a long dark hallway.

The address hadn't had an apartment or room number on it. He pulled out his flashlight and turned it on. The hallway was a straight shot with a few doors off it; two to the right and one to the left, spread out down the hallway. He moved forward and came to the first door. It was secured with a rusty padlock and obviously hadn't been opened in a while.

"What was in this building, Brown?"

"Sir, I'm not sure. Nothing came up when I searched for it."

Dawson frowned, but continued further down. He

reached for his gun and jumped when the front door slammed shut. Brown moved back to the doorway and pushed it open. No one was around. "Just stay there, Brown."

Dawson turned and headed for the next door across the hall. A key lock showed below the doorknob, but when he tried the knob, it didn't turn. Locked. He cursed under his breath. Looking back over his shoulder, Brown stood at the door. One door left. He crept down the hall. He once again ran into a locked door. Damn it.

"Nothing here." He strode down the hall toward Brown.

"What was the point of the addresses then?"

"Damn if I know." Dawson held back the sarcasm, but he was beyond frustrated and had no answers. "What about vic three? Anything new there?"

"Nothing. Diner owner. We found no evidence around him." Brown gestured toward his car. "Want a ride?"

"Sure." Dawson slid into the passenger seat and looked down the street. It was empty. In fact, the surrounding buildings all looked vacant. "Find out what was originally on this street—residential or commercial—and find out what happened to them."

"Yes, sir."

Dawson hid his smirk as he looked out the window. He wouldn't even try to correct him anymore.

twenty-one

Dawson strode into the morgue. He hated this place with a passion—the sterility in smell and looks. It was just cold in all aspects. He shook off the feeling. Although the coldness had always bothered him, lately, he knew he would feel warm as soon as he saw Ali's face. He found her in her office typing up notes.

"Anything on the diner owner?" He spoke as he moved folders from the chair, so he could sit. "Is there ever a time your desk and chairs aren't covered with work?"

Ali scowled at him. "I wish. You know how it is being short-staffed. Damn budget cuts." She took a breath and looked at him. "Well, you look like hell."

"Thanks. What do you have?"

"We already knew who it was. Same weapon—I'd guess an ax or a hatchet—as the others. Far as I could tell, about a dozen blows to the face. Hard to know for sure as they are overlapping. Cuts are deep, right to the bone. I'd say they were carried out with a great deal of force." She leaned back.

Dawson ran a hand over his face, trying to wipe away the tiredness as her brow dipped with concern. "Would you guess a male or a female?"

"Hard to say. From the force of the blows, I'd instinctively say male...but, a female on adrenaline, or with great upper body strength, could probably do that damage, depending on the size of her."

He frowned. "We still have no answers. We went to the first address, and it was nothing but an empty building. Three doors inside, all locked. Brown's searching for the owner."

"What about the other addresses? There were three of them, weren't there?"

He nodded. "The diner was another one. Not sure what that has to do with it. The other one is on the opposite side of the city. I'll go over there next."

"Keep me posted. I'll let you know if anything else comes up as we finish with the diner owner."

Dawson exited the building, drawing in a deep breath. No matter how much time he spent there, he always felt like it was suffocating, despite the warmth he felt when he was in close proximity to Ali.

He jogged back to the station, ran up the stairs, and headed for the victimology board for the third address. He missed the extra staff they used to have. He could use an additional pair of eyes right about now and something to put him ahead of the killer, not two steps behind him or her.

He pulled out a map of the city, hung it on the board, and marked each location with a tack. He shook his head. Nothing stood out as to what the connection was between the three locations. The first had been a dead end, the second the diner. Well, there was only one way to find out what the third one was. He turned on his heel and headed for the unknown.

"Sir...ummm, Dawson?" Brown's voice from behind brought Dawson's attention back to the station.

"What's up, Brown?"

"That address...Chestnut Street...it's owned by O'Shannahan."

"What?" Dawson gestured toward the conference room he'd just vacated. "What other property does he own?"

"I figured you'd ask that, so I did some digging. He owns some other old vacated buildings around the city, but nothing related to the other two addresses."

Dawson stared at the map, where he'd marked the locations. "Good work, Brown. I'm headed to the other address now. Want to ride along?"

"Yes, sir."

Dawson rolled his eyes. "Let's go."

The ride took all of fifteen minutes with the lack of traffic. This city was becoming a ghost town it seemed, and definitely empty as they crossed over to the lower-income area. No renovations had been done in years. Everything looked straight out of a horror movie—abandoned and creepy. Street lights were broken, which would lead to dark streets. And yet, the killings hadn't been done there. Of course, the homeless stayed over where there were more people, and certainly Darla Johnson wouldn't have stepped foot over here. Nor would Finn O'Shannahan, unless he was buying up property to level. But even with his money, Dawson didn't see him building up this end of the city to give it a chance to prosper.

He turned onto Highland Road. "Number eleven is the one we want."

Brown pointed to the right. "Next one, right there."

Dawson pulled the car over and looked at the house. By first appearance, the only word that came to mind was abandoned.

Another dead end?

"Well, let's see if anyone is home." Dawson exited the car and scanned the windows. No sign of life. He pushed open the gate and walked up the walkway…if you could call it that. It had seen better days that was for sure. He walked up the few steps to the front porch. The door knocker was rusty from lack of use. He knocked it and attempted to look through the front windows, but the grime was so thick, he couldn't make out anything other than what looked like a couch.

No answer to his knock. No movement.

"Another dead end. Find out who owns this one and see if you can reach the owner about getting into it." He turned to leave with Brown on his heels. "I'll call O'Shannahan to see if he can get us into the other building."

They were about halfway down the steps when the door creaked open behind them. Dawson turned to see an elderly man peering out.

"Sir, are you the owner here?" Dawson jogged back up the stairs. He showed his badge when he got to the door.

"Yes. What can I do for you?" The man's voice trembled with age.

"What's your name?"

"Name's William Murray." He kept the door barely open enough to look out.

"Do you live here alone, Mr. Murray?" Dawson tried to see past the old man.

"Me and the wife. What do you want?"

"This address was given to me, and I just wanted to check on it. Are you and your wife alone, or do you have family close by?"

The man shook his head. "Our daughter comes to see us some. We're fine." The man started to shut the door.

Dawson held out his business card. "If you ever need anything, just give me a call."

The man grabbed the card, and the door shut before Dawson could say another word. He gestured toward the car, but didn't say anything to Brown until they were sitting in the vehicle.

"Run a check on Mr. William Murray. See if you can find out who his daughter is. Certainly doesn't look like anyone is living there, and definitely not a couple."

There was a feeling to this place that Dawson couldn't put his finger on. The man, the abandoned-looking house…was he looking for an opening in the case in anything at this point?

twenty-two

Days were turning into nights. Life had become a blur for Dawson for the last few days. Had it really been less than a week since this killing spree started? It felt like forever.

He spent nights wandering the alleys looking for his sister and days searching for a lead to get ahead of a killer. He was exhausted, operating on about two-to-three hours of sleep and gallons of coffee. His stomach burned from the amount of caffeine he consumed, as well as the stress he was under. If he got through this investigation without a head full of gray hair, it would be a miracle.

The Leighton police captain, and his own boss, had been riding his ass lately, looking for answers, and yet, the trail seemed cold. There were too many unanswered questions. When he had an opportunity to close his eyes, all he could see were mutilated faces, and his sister's face melding into destruction and blood. The amount of blood in his dreams could wash the whole city away.

He splashed cold water on his face. As he dried off and pulled the towel away, he stared at himself in the mirror. The dark circles under his eyes spoke volumes to his exhaustion; lines furrowed on his forehead showed the stress. As Ali would say, "he looked like hell."

The beep of the coffee maker, indicating it was done brewing, drew him away from the mirror. He fixed his coffee and sat down at his table, pulling a folder close to him. He studied the crime scene for the Borden murders he'd come across while searching the Internet. The face of Andrew Borden was completely unrecognizable. The report had said he'd been struck eleven times in the face. *Eleven.* Seemed like that magical number kept appearing.

Lizzie's story had been contradictory, and there was the issue of her burning her dress, which was considered evidence.

Dawson stared into space. He was drawn back to the addresses given to him. O'Shannahan was still involved in at least one of those addresses, one victim found at the second address and the third—other than the house number being eleven—had turned up with a blatant lack of information. The Murrays were virtually unknown. Brown had done as much digging as he could, but found no birth records for any children. Mary Murray no longer lived in the household, but instead resided at Sunnyside Nursing Home. The stroke she suffered two years ago rendered her unable to speak.

Mr. Murray either didn't remember his wife wasn't living with him any longer, or he was hiding that fact. After seeing him, Dawson leaned toward the man's memory being faulty.

Mind spinning, Dawson ran his fingers through his disheveled hair.

I need a haircut.

The thought caught him off guard. Slamming his hand down on the table, he fought against his mounting frustration. He threw all the printouts back in the folder, dumped his coffee down the drain, and headed for the door.

He'd no sooner walked into the station when Brown approached him.

"Anything new?" Dawson asked.

Brown shook his head. "Not really. Captain's looking for you."

Dawson sighed. Just what he needed—to have his ass chewed out by the captain. He headed into the conference room and saw the man studying the victimology board. He turned to face Dawson as he walked through the door.

"Where did the addresses come from?" The captain spoke without preamble.

"They were left on my car at the cemetery."

"Why were you there?"

Dawson shook his head and turned toward the board. "There was a memorial service for the first victim. I went, hoping to spot someone out of place and possibly getting a lead in the case." He slumped in defeat. "But what I got was a wild-goose chase with these addresses."

The captain studied the board and the map where Dawson had marked the locations. "What do you know about each of these?" He pointed to the thumbtacks on the map.

"One is the diner where the third vic was found...the diner owner actually. This one..." Dawson pointed at another one. "Is an abandoned building owned by O'Shannahan, and the last one is on the other side of the city where an older couple lives. The man can hardly stand up, so I don't see him as a threat."

"O'Shannahan, huh?" The captain shook his head. "That man is a pain in the ass. You'll have to ask him about the property."

"Really? Now I have your permission to question him?"

"You were never told not to, simply to have a reason for it. I'd say you have a reason." His captain gave him a somber look. "Try and do it at his house. Maybe he'll be more receptive."

Dawson nodded. "There's something else."

"What?"

"There's a pattern that resembles a century-old murder. I don't know if there's a correlation or not."

"Okay. What murder?" The captain raised one eyebrow.

"The Lizzie Borden case. She allegedly killed her father and stepmother...with an ax." Dawson watched Captain Collins' face.

The man frowned. "Same weapon on our vics?"

"As far as we can tell without actually finding the thing." Dawson ran a hand across his face in an effort to clear the confusion. He knew he sounded ridiculous, and it probably was a huge leap to go into any of this century-old stuff with Lizzie Borden.

"You're not chasing a ghost, Dawson."

"I know that...but perhaps an obsession that this killer feels the need to copy?" Dawson leaned forward and placed his palms on the table. "What the hell is it then?"

"Go talk to O'Shannahan and see if you can get in that other building. Maybe there are some answers there." Captain Collins laid a hand on Dawson's shoulder. "You'll find the killer. I know you will."

Dawson nodded. The show of support from this man who was hard to read and incredibly stoic gave him a boost in confidence. Still, he questioned, "But will I do it before someone else loses their life?"

twenty-three

The brownstone sat there ominously looking at Dawson, or so it appeared. He took in the shadows covering the doorway. The trees blocked out any hint of light. The darkness matched his mood.

He took the steps two at a time up to the door, drew in a deep breath, and exhaled slowly. The upcoming encounter would not be a pleasant one.

He knocked three times and waited. The door opened slightly. Katie barely peered out, but he recognized her troubled eyes.

"I need to talk to him, Katie," Dawson said sternly.

She pulled the door open wider and stood back for him to enter. Without saying a word, she pointed to the study as she closed the door. Dawson walked to the doorway of the study and stopped. Finn had his back to him, looking out a window.

"Well, what is it this time?" Finn turned to face Dawson.

"I have some questions for you regarding a property you own at 32 Chestnut Street. What can you tell me about that property?" Dawson took a couple steps further into the room, glancing around him. To his right, a floor-to-ceiling bookcase lined the wall. It was filled with books. To the left was a fireplace with a chair sitting next to it. Finn stood over behind his desk and seemed to be taking a minute to formulate an answer.

Dawson casually wandered over to the bookcase and browsed the titles. Classics lined the shelves, from Charles Dickens to self-help books on making millions.

"Chestnut Street?" Finn finally said. "Oh, they were abandoned buildings. I was hoping to develop them into a strip mall." He sat down in his chair and leaned back.

"Have you ever been inside?" Dawson questioned. "Seen inside the locked rooms?"

"Nope. I had no reason to. It had been abandoned for years. If anything's in there, it was from whoever lived there before I bought it. The plan is to just level it."

"I need to get into it. The inside doors are all locked."

Finn's mouth turned up slightly at the corners. "And why would I just let you in my building?"

Dawson stared at him. "I'm asking you to. It could have something to do with the killings, and I need to see what's inside. You just said you have nothing in there, and you don't plan on renovating, so why does it matter?"

"Open myself up so you can try and pin this on me again?" Finn sat forward in his leather chair and just watched Dawson.

Dawson sighed. "No one is trying to pin anything on you, Mr. O'Shannahan. But I'm sure you wouldn't want to obstruct a lead, would you?"

"You realize you've ruined my reputation with that story you leaked to the press." Finn stood up and moved around the desk.

"I leaked? You have quite the imagination. If you don't want to help voluntarily, I can get a court order." Dawson paused briefly. "But if you have nothing to hide, why not just help?"

Finn barked out a laugh. "I don't have anything to hide, detective, but that doesn't mean I need to help you out."

Dawson shrugged and turned toward the door. "Sorry to have bothered you."

"You're giving up that easy?" Finn's voice stopped Dawson at the door. "I would have pegged you for a stubborn fool."

The taunt hit Dawson on his last nerve. He clenched his fists at his sides and took a deep breath. He would *not* be pulled into a battle of the wills. He knew Finn wasn't a killer, but Dawson couldn't rule out his involvement yet, and he refused to be goaded into saying something he'd regret.

He glanced over his shoulder. "There's more than one way to get what I want."

"Is that a threat?"

Dawson smiled. "No, it's a simple reply to your ignorance of how things are done."

Ali had gone over and over every report on all three victims. The only link between them was the blade wounds to their faces and the time of death. Eleven. Eleven wounds, and each victim was killed about 11:00 p.m. What was the significance?

She laid her head on the desk. Exhaustion started to overtake her, and she could only imagine what Wes was going through. She smiled weakly. When did she start thinking of him as Wes instead of Dawson? It went beyond friendship, whether either of them wanted to admit it.

The stress of the madness around the killing spree weighed on everyone involved. The budget cuts had left the precinct and the medical examiner's office short-staffed and those who were left were working overtime to just get through day by day. She felt closed in by these walls. She wanted fresh air and not the stale smell of decaying bodies, formaldehyde, and death. The stench of the dead was everywhere. Even when she was home, the smell lingered on her, no matter how much she showered.

She threw a pad of paper at the wall. Where were the answers? Frustration oozed from her, and a silent scream vibrated through her. They needed a weapon, prints, something to go on. Nothing showed up on tox screens, nor DNA matched any of the victims. Without answers from this office, she was burdened with the feeling of letting Wes down. He needed something to give him hope of finding this sicko.

Maybe it was the stress from the case, but she couldn't help but feel it was more from the strain of trying to avoid the chemistry that obviously sizzled between them. She knew she wasn't the only one who felt it. Otherwise, that kiss wouldn't be haunting her day and night. She'd felt his chemistry for her the other night, yet he still seemed to hold her at arm's length. The damn, "we can't do this," that he threw out there sure didn't help.

Snap out of it, girl. You cannot let him in your head like this. She berated herself for allowing her feelings to bubble to the surface. Yet, she'd never met anyone like Wes, and God help her, she felt like a school girl again every time she saw him.

twenty-four

He was sitting at the kitchen table when I entered the house. He never ventured downstairs without permission. As I leaned against the doorframe, he looked up at me.

"Where is she?"

I smiled. "Where's who?"

"Mary." He looked at his hands. "They came looking for her."

He caught my attention with that. "Who came looking for her?"

He reached for a card on the table. "This young man."

I took the card from his hand and stared at it. Detective Wesley Dawson. How inconvenient. Now I'd need to change my plans. I wanted all this done.

As I stared at the card, a calm settled about me. A flash shot through my memory; a picture that looked so familiar, yet I couldn't place it. Pigeons. I hated the birds, yet I envisioned a coop with a dozen of them inside. The image was gone as quick as it had come, and in its wake, was the start of a migraine.

"Get upstairs," I snapped at the old man.

He stood slowly and shuffled past me. "Where is my Mary?"

"She's dead." The words came out before I thought about it and saw the tears that came to the man's eyes. "Oh, stop your sniveling and get upstairs with your friends. And if you talk to this man again, your daughter, Beth, will soon be with your wife."

I dropped into the chair at the table—the business card still in my hand—and held my head. The pain had become unbearable, and I needed something for it. I reached for a pill bottle in the center of the table, but stopped before I could grab it. Another flash, an ax with blood dripping. I was losing my mind. These weren't my memories. They couldn't be.

As the migraine increased, the voices got louder and louder. I held my head, screaming for the voices to stop. I needed more time. More time to finish what I'd started. I would not fail. No. It wasn't an option. The voices taunted me, telling me I was no good, that I would fail. Yet the flashes continued to show me the way, and despite what I was hearing, I knew I'd done it once before and had gotten away with it, and therefore, I could do it again and again if necessary.

twenty-five

Dawson glanced at the clock. Although he walked in the door just a few minutes ago, he'd changed into dark clothes in record time. Ten o'clock. Later than he usually went out, but it was getting harder and harder to split his time between solving these murders and looking for Sara.

He pulled the black ball cap over his eyes and yanked the hood of his sweatshirt up over it. Truth be told, he was sick of going out every few nights. The search never yielded anything, but guilt consumed him whenever he didn't go. With this killer loose, Dawson was terrified that the next body he'd find would be Sara's, and his nightmares of her mutilated face didn't help the anxiety that racked his body every time a text message came into his phone. He was dreading the next one—the next body he'd have to look at.

He tried to convince himself that these searches were twofold. One to find Sara, but also to hopefully give him some clue to a killer. The homeless provided the perfect place for a cover. He drove to the far side of the city, having never searched the low-income side of town for Sara.

His nerves were frazzled when he parked his car and started walking down a dark street. The streets and alleys were empty. There weren't any homeless on this side of the tracks. As he wandered the streets for two hours, he couldn't tell if he felt relieved to not find anything, or if he was more angered by the fact. On the other side, frustration in not getting any closer to finding Sara tore him apart.

He arrived back home and stopped on his porch steps. The hair on the back of his neck raised, and he could feel eyes on him. He turned slowly around and searched the area in front of his house. It was too dark to see much beyond the porch light. He strained his eyes to look into the darkness, but couldn't see a thing. Still, he felt the presence.

He walked down the steps slowly into the driveway. He stopped at the end of the drive and closed his eyes, relying on his hearing to pick up anything that would give him a clue to who was watching him.

He heard nothing, saw even less. The one thing he was convinced of; he was not in any danger.

He headed back inside and decided to keep the lights off in the house as he moved from window to window to look out. Something caught his eye. Possibly a shadow, but nothing he could tell for sure.

He double-checked the locks on the doors and windows. Although he didn't feel a threat, he wasn't stupid and caution was necessary. It would be a long night, so he settled into a chair by the living room window, completely in the dark, to watch outside.

Dawson stayed awake, looking at the clock for the last time about 5:00 a.m. He woke with a start when his phone rang. 8:00 a.m. Three hours sleep, and in a chair no less. The ache in his neck wasn't about to go away anytime soon. He reached for his phone. Ali.

"Yeah?"

"Is that really the way you answer the phone?" Her teasing came through the line and made him smile.

"You woke me."

"What? At this time? I figured you'd be on the job already."

He stood and stretched. "Didn't get much sleep last night. I'm burning the candle at both ends, and it's starting to catch up with me. I need some answers and a break in all areas."

"No luck with Sara?"

He smiled. "No. And you think that's my top priority?"

"I didn't say it was your top priority, but I know she's right up there, and I also know you're worried even more about her with this killer on the loose."

He nodded, although he knew she couldn't see him. "I just felt like someone was watching me last night. Not really a threat, but I got home at midnight and just sensed it."

"Are you safe there?"

He chuckled. "You realize I can take care of myself?"

"I don't doubt that...but as macho as you like to think you are, exhaustion can make you more of a target. And don't even try to deny it."

"You think I'm macho?" He teased.

"Do you want coffee this morning?"

"What? You're not going to answer me?" He knew he should let it go, but all he could think about was the taste of her lips and how he wanted more of her.

"Wes..."

"Yes?"

Ali giggled. "You said we can't." She hung up the phone before he could reply.

Dawson shook his head. Had he been the one to set that boundary? Was she giving him the option to change it?

133

He headed to the shower. It would have to be a cold one after hearing Ali's voice, but it was worth it. He needed to solve this crime, and then maybe, just maybe, he would have a taste of her again.

Dawson ran up the precinct steps. The cold shower had definitely woken him up, but did nothing to squelch the ache that was increasing for Ali. He arrived at his desk to find a steaming cup of coffee waiting for him with a small note attached: About time you showed up.

He shook his head with a grin.

Brown came up behind him and cleared his throat.

Dawson smiled, recognizing Brown's usual tentativeness to talk to him. "Yup, whatcha got?" Dawson spoke, never turning around. He sipped his coffee while waiting for the answer.

"Sir, the Murrays have one daughter."

Dawson turned to face him. "Anyone we know?"

"Elizabeth Murray, sir. Only child of Mary and William Murray."

Dawson shook his head. "That's it?"

Brown smiled. "No, sir. Mary had a brother."

"Is that important, Brown?"

"Yes, sir. Her brother was vic three, Charlie." Brown grinned at him.

"Wait…Elizabeth. Beth, the waitress, is their daughter?"

"Yes, sir."

Dawson rolled his eyes. "Please, Brown. Stop with the sir." He sipped his coffee again. "Get me Beth's address."

Brown turned on his heel and was gone before Dawson could say another word. This was an interesting turn of events. Maybe the break he'd been hoping for. He settled into his chair and enjoyed his coffee for a moment before setting it aside.

He signed into his computer. First things first. He opened a Google page and typed in Lizzie Borden, "11" and hit search. The same information popped up that he'd found before. He was nowhere closer to finding any information that would lead him to the killer and the frustration was palpable around him.

twenty-six

Another Saturday came around. Dawson had been over-extending himself between the case and his nightly searches for his sister, and he was exhausted. For the first time since the killing spree had started, he shut his alarm off and prayed sleep would carry him through the night. His slumber had been filled with nightmares—more of the same—and then an uneasy rest.

He woke with the sun shining in his window and glanced at the clock beside the bed. 8:00 a.m. Well, at least, he had slept a bit last night. He rolled over to his side and punched the pillow down, closing his eyes to catch a few more winks.

His phone beeped quietly. Had he been sleeping, he wouldn't have heard it, but being awake, he was unable to ignore it. He reached for it. A few emails, which he disregarded and checked the text messages. Two unread. One was from Ali and the other from one of his sisters who he hadn't talked to in years. *Please call.* Two simple words.

He stared at the phone. After all this time, his sister

texts him with only two words. Was he supposed to jump and do her bidding immediately? Part of him wanted to balk at the urge to call her, but the other part, with all the stress of the killings, couldn't be ignored. It might be important.

What's wrong? He typed back, then threw his phone on the nightstand and sat up on the side of the bed. He stared off into space, running through options of what he needed to do, or should do today. He really didn't want to go into work and look at another dead end. Maybe a day away would do him some good.

His phone beeped with a text. *Have you heard from Sara?*

No, have you? He texted back. The hairs on the back of his neck stood on edge. Why after all these years was his older sister asking about Sara? She'd cut all ties and wanted nothing to do with Dawson or their parents.

Heard about murders. Just thought of her.

Dawson sighed. He couldn't deny that it wouldn't be unusual for his sister to worry also, even if they had cut ties. Family was family and when things were tough, they still worried about each other, and he'd made sure they all had his number in case they needed him.

None of them are her. I'm still looking for her.

Keep me posted. That was it. End of conversation.

He didn't even bother replying. Instead, he headed to the shower to try and clear the fog from his mind. Leaning into the water, he stood still and allowed the water to rain over him. The hot steam circled around him much like the fog in his mind swirled around the unknown just out of his reach.

Feeling a bit clearer-minded, he shut off the water. He reached for his towel and stopped, then listened intently for a few moments. Shaking his head, he chided himself for being paranoid.

He dressed quickly and headed for the kitchen.

Again, thinking he heard a bang, he bypassed the kitchen and made his way to the front door. The screen door was swinging loosely, which was unusual since he knew he latched it last night when he'd come home.

He unlocked and opened the front door to catch the screen door. Looking down, he noticed a small rock on top of a piece of paper. He reached for it, and looked around as he picked it up. Nothing appeared to be out of the ordinary, so he relatched the screen door, shut and locked the front door, and carried the piece of paper into the kitchen.

He stopped next to the table and glanced down at his hand. He held the paper between his thumb and forefinger, *delicately*, like it would break if he were to move it too quickly. But he didn't move it at all. He simply stared at it, feeling no urgency to open it. Instead, he quelled his curiosity and simply waited.

His mind ran through the possibilities of what it was and why it was on his step. Typically, Sara would lodge her notes in the doorjamb. He had the distinct impression his door was left unlatched to draw his attention.

Sighing, he pulled out a chair and sat down, opening the note. The handwriting was Sara's…he would bet his life on it. There was no S signing it, but the simple words, *Don't overthink it. The answer is right in front of you.*

He looked it over, front and back, and that was it. He closed his eyes and pinched his fingers against the bridge of his nose. How much more could he take of this? Sara was close by, he had known this for years, but her elusiveness was starting to grate on him. Why was she hiding from him?

His stomach twisted and churned with the increased anxiety. What answer? Was he overthinking finding Sara? Finding the killer? *Both?* He had no idea what this note referred to, and he threw it on the table in disgust. Nothing but another dead end for both problems.

He glanced at the coffee maker and thought about

making some, but instead, grabbed his phone and headed for the door. He stood on the front steps and looked around. The neighbor across the street was still away on their yearly month-long vacation. Their house appeared abandoned, although Wes knew that every night at different times various lights would come on with timers, giving the impression someone was home.

He kept an eye out on the place when they were gone, but lately he'd been preoccupied and hadn't thought of the owners being away. He jogged across the street and walked around the house. He checked doors and windows and saw nothing was amiss. Satisfied he hadn't been missing anything with his inattentiveness to the place, he turned toward his house once more.

He walked past the detached garage. Out of the corner of his eye, he noticed a brief movement. Turning to look behind the shrubs next to the building, he found a yellow tabby cat watching him. As he moved closer, it meowed at him before turning and running away. Dawson shrugged and scolded himself for being paranoid once more.

He felt like he was in a cat and mouse game, and that the actual cat he just saw was taunting him. Between the killer and looking for Sara, he was two steps behind every time. Sara would leave him notes, but he never could catch her. The killer eluded him every moment. He needed to find a way to get ahead of both of them, and to get them off the streets.

He turned right and headed in the opposite direction of the city. He lived not far from downtown, but to the other side of him was the Atlantic Ocean. Leighton was twenty-five miles east of New Haven. Although Dawson worked mostly out of Middleton, the headquarters for the state police, he lived in Leighton and had for years. He loved the fact that he was close enough to work on the coast. The rocky coastline was often his source of stress relief when he could get away. Today, he needed to do just that, and a walk on the beach was exactly what was in order.

He picked his way down the rocks to get to the shoreline. This was an area of the coast that wasn't often visited by people; certainly, no tourists came this far inland away from the sandy beach area. It was rocky, but when it was low tide, it was a great place to walk between the water and the rocks.

He moved slowly, focusing in on the sound of the waves lapping at the beach. The salt air filled his senses, and a feeling of peace came over him. The stress of the case, and of not finding Sara, released from his shoulders, and for the first time since the killing spree started, he felt like his mind was clear and he could think unobstructed.

He sat down on a cluster of rocks and stared out over the water. The horizon was clear and the blue of the sky met the edge of the ocean and blended so perfectly—the setting he'd been needing for days now. Yet as much as he craved this peacefulness, he also did his best thinking here.

He forced his mind to return to the case. He closed his eyes and pictured Eugene lying in the alley—his blood blending with the asphalt, slashes to his face melding into each other. Dawson's thoughts moved to Darla, the second victim. She had the same blending of blood and mutilation, just like Charlie. Dawson pushed and pushed his mind to see a connection. What was he missing? O'Shannahan connected to two of the victims, but not to Charlie or the diner that Dawson could discern.

His phone beeped with a text and he opened his eyes. *Where are you? Brought you breakfast.*

He smiled. *Ali.*

At Leighton's Point. Come join me.

There was no response. Instinctively, he knew that Ali was on her way. She'd become a solid constant in his life through this mess, professionally and personally. She never questioned his actions about searching for Sara, but was always concerned about him and what the search took from him. There was no judgment, just friendly concern. He was getting used to her silent support of him, and he found himself wondering what life was like before he'd met her. They'd been thrown together through these murders, and yet, he couldn't remember her not being there.

"Wow, this is great here. I've never been down this far." Ali's voice broke through his musings, and he turned to look at her, then stood and held out his hand to help her over the rocks.

"It's a good place to think. One I used to frequent, but lately have been too preoccupied to get here."

"Well, maybe it's just the place you need to be right now." She handed him a bag and a coffee. He opened the bag and found fresh donuts from the local bakery.

"Thank you." He held out the bag to her, then waited until she grabbed one before diving in himself to taste the warmth of the straight-from-the-oven donuts. "Nothing better than a warm donut and the sound of the ocean."

Ali nodded. She sat silently beside him, watching the waves. "What do you think about when you're here?" she finally asked.

"In the past, I spent a lot of time here wondering about Sara and how she could have left me in the dark like she has. This morning, the murders are more on my mind and trying to figure out what it is I'm missing."

"What did you come up with?"

He shrugged. "Not a thing."

"Okay. We know the victims themselves aren't related or connected in any way, except by the diner."

He nodded. "But that's a dead end."

"Is it?" She prodded. "Think about the diner. What else does it connect with?"

He stood and started pacing. "There's Amy, the missing waitress who disappeared just before the first murder. And Beth, the unpopular waitress, who I just found out is the daughter of the couple at the third address that was given to me."

"Wait. She's connected to the third address?"

Yes. I stopped by there. The old man doesn't seem to be all there upstairs. He said he and his wife lived there, but his wife is in a nursing home." Dawson turned and looked at Ali.

"I just want to know who gave you those addresses? Is it to throw you off, or is it because they truly are connected to the case?" Ali mused.

"You've got me. None of it seems to make much sense. There are connections between two of them, and connections between another two, but nothing connects all three." He sat back down next to her. "So, what are we missing?"

"I don't know." She shivered a little as the wind picked up, and she moved a bit closer to him. Instinctively, he wrapped his arm around her, attempting to shield her from the cold.

"Why don't we get out of this wind?" He stood and pulled her up with him. "Back to my place?"

"Is your car here?"

"I walked this morning."

She nodded. "Well, come on then."

He kept a tight grip on her hand, helping her back up the rocks. The heat from their touch shot up his arm, and he wanted nothing more than to just stay here in this peacefulness and enjoy her company. If not for the icy wind . . .

She unlocked her car and he waited patiently while she cleaned off the passenger seat from files and empty water bottles. "No judgments about my car."

He laughed. "I would expect it to be just like your office."

He sat in silence while she drove. He felt comfortable in the silence—something that didn't usually happen—and he pondered how someone could have such a positive impact in his life in all the little ways, after only knowing each other such a short time. He sneaked a peek at her out of the corner of his eye and admired the simple beauty of her.

twenty-seven

Ali and Dawson arrived at his place. As they entered the kitchen, she pointed at the note he'd left on the table. "What's this?"

"You got me. I found it on my doorstep. It's in Sara's handwriting, but she didn't sign it like she normally does."

"What do you mean?"

He walked over to the desk in the hallway and pulled out all the notes Sara had left him and handed them to Ali. "She usually signs it with an S, but not this time. Still, I swear it's the same handwriting. But I have no idea what she's talking about…what's right in front of me?"

Ali slid into a chair and looked over all the notes. "She's keeping an eye on you. She knows you're out searching for her."

"Yeah. But why not just come to me and talk?"

"She must have her reasons. But, at least, she's letting you know she's safe."

"Safe?" He scoffed. "That's a relative term, isn't it, with a lunatic running around killing people?

Ali smiled. "You know what I mean. I understand you're frustrated, but there isn't anything you can do about Sara if she doesn't want you to find her."

"I know," he admitted defeat. "But I don't have to like it."

Ali rolled her eyes. "Okay, what else about the case? What's your next move?"

He sat back. "I need to find Amy, the other waitress who conveniently disappeared. Her apartment has been empty, but I'm going to try and talk to the neighbors again. She couldn't have just vanished into thin air."

"You wouldn't think so," Ali agreed.

"Now that the diner is closed, where are all the regulars going?" He sat up. "Is there another restaurant, or diner maybe, that's benefiting from Charlie's death. Maybe that's a place to start."

"Okay, but how do you find that out. In Leighton, how many restaurants are there?"

He reached for his phone and started searching. "In the same area, only a couple really. I'd think Charlie's regulars would want to stay around there and go to a place with the same type and pricing of food, which narrows it down to one. Sally's Kitchen. It's two blocks over from Charlie's."

"Hungry? Maybe we should check it out for lunch?"

He grinned. "I'm always hungry."

Deciding to drive, Dawson and Ali jumped into his car. They arrived at the diner just before lunch rush. The inside was nothing at all like Charlie's. Tables were updated and clean, the floor sparkled, and there was an open, airy atmosphere. They chose a table near the back, where they could see people coming and going.

"Definitely cleaner than Charlie's," Dawson remarked.

"Well, let's hope the food is spectacular," Ali said as she perused the menu.

"Can I start you with some drinks?" A waitress appeared next to their table. She had her blond hair pulled back in a ponytail and was dressed in a classic pink and white diner uniform. She smiled at them and waited patiently.

"Iced tea, for me," Ali answered.

"Water with lemon, please." Dawson looked up. "What do you recommend for lunch?"

"We have the usual sandwiches, but my personal favorite is the open-faced hot roast beef sandwich. Sally makes her own gravy."

"That sounds good to me," he said.

"I'll have the same," Ali chimed in.

"Great. I'll be right back with your drinks." The waitress moved away as quietly as she had arrived.

He glanced around. A few tables were filled. The walls were covered with pictures of Leighton from years ago. Memorabilia from shops that had long closed was scattered about. A picture of the train station caught his eye, and he stood to go get a closer look. The train station had been torn down years ago, but it still delineated the two sides of the city. The picture was taken so the rough side of town was in the background. Not much had changed as far as buildings. They still looked as dilapidated back then as they did now. Apparently, the *wrong side of the tracks* had always been a clear definition.

He returned to the table. "Even hundreds of years ago, one side of this city was always run down. I wonder if there was ever a time that it was just a fluid city, no wrong side or right side, up and coming, or run down?"

"It's kind of sad that there's always a line drawn in the sand between the rich and the poor," Ali mused.

He glanced up and smiled, acknowledging the waitress as she returned with their drinks. "Thank you."

"Are things busier these days with Charlie's being shut down?" Dawson asked.

The waitress nodded. "It's definitely been good for

business, but we didn't suffer when he was open. Sally and Charlie are very different owners and cooks."

Dawson looked around. "Have you worked here long?"

The waitress smiled. "Since I was a teenager. I'm Kara. This has been a family-owned and run business forever. Sally is my great aunt."

"What have you heard about Charlie's closing?" Dawson probed.

"Just that he'd been murdered behind the diner. Nothing else really. People haven't talked much about it, at least not when I'm in earshot." Kara tapped their table. "I'll be back with your sandwiches in a few minutes."

Ali smirked at him. "Is there ever a time you can enjoy a meal without interrogating the help?"

"Not until I've caught this sicko." He knew she was kidding, but it was a sharp reminder that even on his days off he was still very much on the job.

Sandwiches arrived, and they ate in silence, just enjoying the hot, delicious food in front of them. After they finished, he sat back and scanned the room again. "Definitely better food than Charlie's."

"So much better. I can't believe I've never tried this place before. I loved Charlie's omelets, but now I'm wondering if I'd been going to the wrong place all along."

Dawson laughed. "Who would have thought that looking for a killer would lead us to incredible food."

Kara arrived back at their table to clear their plates. "I take it you enjoyed it."

"It was great," Ali answered.

"Dessert? Sally just took an apple pie out of the oven about an hour ago. It's still warm, and I can put some vanilla ice cream on it."

Dawson looked at Ali, and she nodded. "Two, please," he answered. As Kara moved away with their dirty plates, he returned his attention to Ali. "I couldn't eat here often, unless I was working out three times a day to get rid of the weight I'd put on."

She gave him the once over. "I think you could maintain that physique no matter what you ate." The flirting was subtle, but it was there and he had no doubt that this could lead to complications, but he didn't care at the moment. He enjoyed Ali's company too much to not flirt, especially when all he wanted to do was take her in his arms and kiss her senseless.

Ali watched Wes look at the pictures and talk to the waitress. He was always on duty regardless if it was off hours or not. She admired the way he handled himself and picked up on details such as in pictures that most people wouldn't even look at. He had an eye for details and she had noticed him teaching that skill to Officer Brown. She smiled faintly as the thought of him being gruff with Brown simply because he called him sir, yet the way he was patient with him in teaching him observation skills.

He was so multi-layered and she was privileged to be able to see more and more of those layers. She caught herself feeling proud of him. A proudness that she would only feel for someone she truly cared about.

And to sit here and admire the man's body. She had no idea where he put all the food he ate, but oh, those muscles could make her weak in the knees.

twenty-eight

Sunday morning came, and Dawson, refreshed from having some time off the day before, found himself on the way to the police station. He acknowledged the skeleton crew on duty, and once again, he was struck by how the economy had affected everyone. Every location was short-staffed these days, and especially the smaller precincts. Luckily, working for the state police afforded him a bit more resources to work with.

He made his way to the conference room to study the victimology board. He viewed each victim and the links that had been tied to them. He was still missing Amy, the other waitress. He located her address in the file, and decided with it being Sunday, maybe he'd get lucky and find her home, or at least some neighbors who might know something.

The address was only a few blocks from the diner, not in the worst section of town, but definitely in the run-down portion of the better side of the city. As he entered the apartment building, he heard a baby crying. He couldn't tell if it came from the first floor or from the one above. He shook his head and wondered how these tenants could stand hearing every single noise their neighbors made.

He made his way to the stairs and the second floor. Amy's apartment was 205. The dark and dingy hallway had only two working light bulbs, one at each end of it. The bulb nearest Amy's apartment was burnt out and in need of replacement.

Dawson knocked on the door and waited. He rapped again and finally heard some movement. The door cracked open.

"Yes?" a female voice asked.

"Amy Patterson?" He held up his badge so she could see it.

The door opened just a bit more. "I'm Amy."

He glanced past her into the apartment. Dishes littered the countertop and filled the sink. "May I come in?"

"I'm sorry. I've been sick and I'm still not feeling well. I'd hate for you to catch what I have." She blocked the door, but opened it enough to carry on a conversation with him.

"Sorry to hear that. How long have you been sick?"

"A couple of days now." She shrugged. "I'd been visiting family out of town. Guess I picked it up there."

"When did you get back?"

"Last Tuesday. Why?"

He watched her carefully. "Miss, Charlie is dead and there have been two others who were regulars at the diner who've also been killed. I need to get some insight into these people and their habits."

With a look of surprise, Amy took a step back. "Ignore the mess. I need to sit down." She turned and walked into the living room.

Dawson quietly closed the door behind him as he followed her into the apartment. The small place was a mess.

He stood in the space between the living room and the kitchen, surrounded by filth. The kitchen sink was piled high with dirty dishes that obviously had been there for weeks. The floor at the end of the kitchen was sticky, and Dawson tried not to grimace. The smell of stale air and sickness assaulted his senses and he prayed he wouldn't see any cockroaches. He stifled a shudder and waited for Amy to say something.

She sat down on a small love seat. "I liked Charlie a lot. I hated working with Beth though. She was just miserable."

"When was the last day you worked?" Dawson asked. "Charlie mentioned that you'd just not showed up one day."

"Ha. That's nice. No, Charlie had been out, and I was headed out of town to visit family. I told Beth to pass the message on to him. Apparently, she didn't bother to."

Dawson made a mental note to question Beth next. "What do you know about a homeless man named Eugene?"

Amy smiled. "He was the sweetest man. He came in every morning and sat with Mr. Floyd, who bought him breakfast. Every day like clockwork. Is Eugene okay?" She looked up at Dawson with panic in her eyes.

He shook his head. "I'm sorry to say, he was our first victim."

Amy's eyes filled with tears. "That poor sweet man. Did someone tell his daughter? I didn't know her, but he talked about her all the time."

"Yes, she was told." Dawson gave her a moment to compose herself. "Do you know Darla Johnson?"

Amy frowned. "She wasn't very nice. I mean, she treated me okay, but she was really cruel to Beth. Honestly, I never could figure out why she'd come to the diner. She was always dressed to the nines. She didn't seem to fit in there, and that perfume...enough to choke ya." Amy grimaced for a minute before her eyes widened. "Oh, no. Her, too?"

He nodded. "Yes, second victim. Then Charlie. He died behind the diner."

"I don't know how I can help you. I never had a problem with any of those people. Beth was hard to work with, but no one treated her very well either. I suppose it's hard to be pleasant when everyone is against you." Amy shrugged.

"Did any of these three, Eugene, Darla or Charlie, have any problems with anyone else who came in?"

"Nah. Charlie was, well, Charlie was Charlie. He was gruff and stayed in the kitchen most of the time. He didn't bother anyone. Just did his job and let us do ours. Eugene, everyone loved. Darla, well she didn't fit in, but everyone talked with her. She was pushy. She just got her real estate license and was pushing people to call her and refer her."

Dawson smiled. "Thank you, Amy." He laid his business card down on the coffee table in front of her. "Call me if you think of anything else."

"I will."

He left the apartment while Amy stayed seated. He'd gotten no answers from her, but she'd confirmed what he already knew. There was no real connection between the victims except the diner. Another dead end.

He sat in his car and took in the run-down building surrounded by others that were very much just as dilapidated. This was the section of town that Finn O'Shannahan was buying up. Dawson sent a text to Brown to check into the apartment building ownership. He'd lay money down that Finn owned this one, too.

It was time to get that court order to see the inside of the other building. The one Finn had refused them entry. Dawson needed a connection between the three addresses left to him. He was still haunted by who'd put the envelope on his windshield and couldn't help but wonder if he was on a wild-goose chase.

By the time he returned to the police station, Brown

had shown up and gave him the name of a holding company that owned the apartment building Amy lived in. Unfortunately, there was no link to O'Shannahan.

Frustration gripped Dawson. "Do we know who owns the holding company?"

"No, sir," Brown replied. "I couldn't get that information."

Dawson nodded as he strode out of the conference room. As he made his way to the parking lot, his thoughts turned to questioning Beth. Sliding into the driver's seat, he turned his car toward the other side of the city and headed back to 11 Highland Road, home of the Murray's. He parked across the street and studied the ramshackle residence. There were no signs of life. The windows looked like they had the last time he was there—filthy and no light shining through. In fact, the whole house looked to be abandoned.

He decided to approach the house and reached for the car door handle, when he caught a glimpse of someone making their way up the sidewalk. He sat back and waited. He watched as Beth Murray opened the gate to the walkway that led to the house.

He exited the car and jogged across the street. "Beth."

She turned toward him, irritation shadowing her face. "Yes?"

"This is your parents' home, correct?"

"You know that already. My dad said you stopped here before." She made no move to continue up the walkway to the house.

"I had a couple of questions for him. Is he around to talk to?"

She glanced at her watch. "My father isn't well, and this is the time he's typically napping. Is there something I can help you with?"

"Not well?" Dawson questioned.

"Detective, my father is delusional and has been since

my mother was moved to a nursing home. He doesn't even know who he is most days." Beth tapped her foot. "Is there really a need to talk with him?"

Dawson watched her carefully. "Do you live here with him?"

"No, I don't. I stop by regularly to check on him, but he has a nurse who stays nights with him." Beth half-turned. "If there's nothing else…"

Dawson reached out his hand to stop her. "Actually, I have a few questions for you."

Beth sighed. "What?"

"Shall we go inside?"

"Nope. Ask right here." She still didn't make eye contact with him.

"Fine. Why didn't you tell Charlie that Amy had to go out of town?"

Beth shifted from foot to foot. "Don't know. Didn't really care if she was there or not."

"You let Charlie think she had just stopped showing up. Why?" Dawson pressed.

Beth clenched her hands by her thighs. "I really could care less what Charlie thought of her. She was a bitch to me, just like everyone else there. Is that what you want to hear?"

Dawson stood quietly for a second. "I'm going to want to talk to you again, so stay close by."

He watched Beth climb the steps to the front door, where she paused and turned to look at him, obviously waiting for him to leave. He walked slowly in the direction of his vehicle. The instant he heard the door open, he spun to get a glimpse inside just as she was closing the door, but he couldn't see a thing due to the darkness in the house.

Swearing under his breath, he went back to his car.

twenty-nine

Monday rolled around and Dawson arrived at the station bright and early. After yesterday's meetings with Amy and Beth, he was convinced that he was missing the connection. He had yet to get a search warrant for the abandoned building owned by Finn, and without Finn's cooperation, it was a moot point. Dawson was frustrated with the lack of progress, and his boss was breathing down his neck, partly due to Captain Collins at the local department complaining about him upsetting the flow of the precinct.

Dawson was trying more and more to stay out of the building and only come in to go over the victimology board when necessary. He grabbed the file and looked again through the pictures from the three crime scenes. Laying them out on the table, side by side, the similarities were uncanny. The one difference was the second victim. Her face looked as if the perp had been in a rage as opposed to the other two. What made this particular victim provoke that kind of response? Was she known to the killer, or was it a random thing?

He shuffled the pictures together and placed them in

the folder, then pulled out the paper with the addresses on it. He'd made notes on it as to the owners and what he'd found when the properties had been visited. The Sunnyside Nursing Home note caught his eye. That was his next stop.

Grabbing the folder, he headed for the door. The nursing home was on the outskirts of town. As he drove up the winding driveway to the parking lot, he took in the view. The nursing home had been built up on a hill that overlooked the city. To the back of the building was the edge of a wooded area. The front and sides were unobstructed, and each angle had an exceptional view.

He stopped at the nursing station. "Excuse me, can you tell me what room Mary Murray is in?"

The nurse turned and looked him up and down. "May I ask who you are? Mary doesn't get many visitors."

He fished out his ID. "I just have a few questions for her."

The nurse came around the counter and gestured for him to follow her. "She's down this way, room 111. You realize Mrs. Murray is nonverbal?"

He shook his head. "No, I didn't know. Can she communicate at all?"

"I'll go in with you. I can usually understand a few things from her. She doesn't write anymore. Her stroke left her paralyzed on the right side. She never was very legible writing with the left hand."

She pushed open the door to Room 111, and lying in the bed was an elderly woman. Her wrinkled hands and arms—as thin as a rail—lay at her sides on the outside of her covers. The blanket had been pulled up to her chest, and she stared up at the ceiling.

"Mrs. Murray, you have company." The nurse was upbeat and made every effort to exude cheer, but her patient stared blankly and didn't respond to her.

"Mrs. Murray, I'm Detective Dawson. Mind if I ask

you a few questions?" He stood close by her bed. Her eyes turned toward him, and she blinked twice.

"Two blinks mean yes," the nurse explained.

He nodded. "Mrs. Murray, do you know where you are?" Two blinks.

"Does your daughter, Beth, come to visit you often?" One blink. He looked at the nurse and she shook her head, confirming the negative response.

"Do you see your husband often?"

One blink.

"No one comes these days to see her," the nurse whispered.

"Thank you, Mrs. Murray. I appreciate your time." Dawson patted her hand and turned to leave.

The nurse followed him out into the hallway. "Her husband only came a couple of times, then Beth stopped bringing him, and she never comes. She didn't like bringing her father anyway. I don't even know where he is these days."

Dawson frowned. "When Beth came with her father, did she visit with her mother at all, or just bring him and leave?"

"Oh, she stayed. Watched her father like a hawk. By the time Mary was placed here, her stroke had already rendered her nonverbal."

"Thank you for your time." Dawson left the building, curious, but not really surprised at Beth's attitude toward her parents. She seemed to have that general attitude with everyone.

Anxiety welled inside of me, and I paced the small room. Things were not going smoothly. I had an itch to finish up the last couple of names, yet that damn detective was mucking things up. Back and forth across the room, my hands gesturing as I silently tried to figure out my next step.

I stopped beside the small table and picked up my list. Two names left, then it would be over. I'd be free.

I yanked open the closet door. The black cloak—clean once again—hung with my black gloves on the shelf right above it. I ran a hand over the dark garments and closed my eyes at the memories of the power that had run through me with every blow of the hatchet.

Suddenly a face came into my mind; a woman I didn't know. I opened my eyes and looked around. I felt I should know who she was. She was laughing and scolding me at the same time. But I didn't know her, so why was her face in my mind?

The intrusion into my blissful memories agitated me, and I reached for the cloak. Did I dare strike again tonight? I smoothed the cloak down as I settled the hood around my face. Pulling on the gloves, I listened carefully at the door. Hearing nothing, I crept down the hall into the alley. It was dark tonight, no moon. Rain was supposedly coming in and there wouldn't be many people on the streets. Even the homeless would be huddled under some cardboard and not wandering around like usual.

I moved quickly to my car and drove out of the city on backroads. Meeting no other cars, my anticipation heightened. The hatchet lay waiting under my seat. These next two names were the crux of all my problems, and once they were gone, freedom would be mine.

I took an old logging road to the section of woods behind the nursing home. That detective had been an irritant to me for far too long, and if he wasn't careful, I'd veer from my original plan and just start knocking off other people just to keep him busy. The thought brought a smile to my face and I lingered on it for a moment. I shook my head. I had a deliberate plan, and I needed to keep to it. No other killings just for the fun of it. Although I enjoyed it so much—the warm blood, the sight of terror in their eyes, especially when they recognized me—but I wasn't the kind of killer who killed for the pleasure. There was a reason for my victims to suffer the way they did.

I left the car, weapon in hand, and picked my way through the wooded area. I fled across the small open space between the woods and the building. Pressed against the building, in the shadows, I moved cautiously around to the window I knew so well. How many nights had I sat outside this window and just watched her? The one who should've been my protector and instead had been part of the nightmare?

The family had requested this room that had doors to a patio so she could look outside from her bed. She loved flowers, and the nursing staff had kept potted purple and pink pansies on the patio for her. I peeked inside. The room was dark except for a small light coming from the bathroom. She appeared to be sleeping.

I looked at my watch. Almost eleven. The witching hour for me. I gripped the handle of the hatchet and let the hardness of the wood encourage me. I slowly twisted the lever of the door. I'd visited this place so regularly and fixed the locking mechanism so that it didn't always click into a locked position. It was undetectable, really, since the nursing staff wasn't always on the ball. For most of the nurses, it was just a paycheck and they treated the patients as such. That's how I knew entering this room at night would be no problem. I carefully inched the door open and crept across the floor to the side of the bed. I listened intently for any sound that would indicate someone was approaching. It was silent.

Eerily silent.

I looked down at the patient and found her watching me. Recognition in her eyes. No terror, just sadness. No, she needed to be afraid of me. I leaned over and put my face close to hers. "Do you know why I'm here?"

I pulled back so I could see her face clearly. She blinked twice. Damn. She still wasn't afraid. "Are you prepared to die?"

She reached for my hand, and I allowed her to touch me. She squeezed, trying to convey something. I had no idea what it was she wanted to say. Her eyes were tear-filled, and I couldn't tell if it was fear or sadness that overcame her.

Talking came from down the hall, changing everything. I turned and sprinted from the room, careful to shut the door behind me as quietly as I had opened it.

Racing across the open area to the woods, I stopped against a tree in the shadows and watched the building for a moment. That woman—why wasn't she afraid of me? She had tortured me all my life. I'd been scared to death of her growing up. Why couldn't the tables be turned this time?

The agony of feeling like a failure hit me. No, I would not allow it to overtake me.

I hurried to my car and drove back to my place. Once inside, I returned the cloak and gloves to their spot in the closet. I sat on the bed, leaning forward with my hands covering my face. The terror of my youth started to have a hold on me. I wept silently, praying it wouldn't happen again.

As memories of my childhood flooded over me, the sensations and smells were strong, like it was happening at that very moment. Then a face flashed in front of me that I didn't recognize, but it wasn't the woman from before.

I scrambled farther up on the bed, my back flat against the wall. Who was that coming at me? As quick as the memory had appeared, it was gone.

Tears rolled down my face, and I was shaking uncontrollably. And as soon as the memory faded, the throbbing pain in my head started. I laid down on the small bed and pulled the thread-bare blanket over me, praying sleep would overtake me quickly.

thirty

Dawson made his way down to the basement of the Medical Examiner's building, down the hall to Ali's office. He stopped just outside the door and watched her. She sat furiously scribbling notes and signing documents. The pile in front of her never seemed to diminish, only appeared to have increased every time he came into this office.

"Are you going to come in or just watch me from the door?" Ali's voice broke his thoughts. She never looked up and continued to write.

"How do you do that?" He walked in and cleared the chair, holding the files.

She flashed him a grin. "You're saying you can't tell when you're being watched, Mr. Brilliant Detective?"

"Very cute." He gestured to the files. "Do you ever make progress on these things?"

"Come on. You know how it is. Do the files on your desk ever diminish?"

He knew the answer, and so did she. It was the business they were in. Crimes never stopped, nor did dead bodies. And when crimes couldn't get solved right away, things piled up even quicker.

"Well, what's new on the case?" Her voice refocused his mind.

"Not much really. I visited Mary Murray at the nursing home. She's nonverbal, so no information coming there. Just her husband and daughter don't visit her." He shrugged. "Maybe that's not that strange. I mean, her husband seems senile, and he's not even aware his wife doesn't live with him."

"Did you find out where Beth was living?"

He shook his head. "Can't get any information on her. Her legal address is still her parents' home. Maybe she technically still lives there and just doesn't spend much time there. You know as well as me that she isn't very forthcoming with answers."

"I feel bad for her," Ali sympathized. "I think she's one of those people that because she's quiet has been bullied her whole life. You saw the way customers treated her at Charlie's."

"I know. And I added to that by baiting her. Even Charlie wasn't nice to her that first time I talked to him. I know she was worried about the place shutting down and not being able to pay her bills."

"Another innocent victim in the fallout of this damn serial killer."

He concurred. Ali had a good insight to a lot of things, and he knew he wasn't always a people person and didn't look at them like she did. She was good for him, in more ways than not. "What do you say we get some dinner tonight? Something other than diner food?"

She smiled and leaned back in her chair. "What did you have in mind?"

"How about The Log Cabin in Clinton?"

"That place is fabulous. Sounds good."

He stood and placed the files back in the chair. "I'll pick you up at six?"

She nodded and went back to her pile of papers. He smiled. They both were obsessed with their job and never took much time away. Dinner would be a nice change of pace for them. Until then, he had a few more hours to make some headway in this case.

He jogged across the street to the station and again went to study the victimology board. He grabbed a pad of paper and started listing people he'd talked to and crossed off those that he had cleared from being involved.

Finn O'Shannahan was still at the top of the list. He was uncooperative and continued to block Dawson from searching the inside of that abandoned building. He looked at the other addresses: the diner and the Murray's house. Neither of them held any clues. The Murray's was a dilapidated place, much like O'Shannahan's building. Charlie's wasn't completely run down, but it wasn't in the best shape either. Maybe that was the key? Was Finn trying to buy up the other two places, too? Was that the connection?

"Anything new?" Captain Collin's voice came from behind him.

Dawson groaned. "Nothing." He passed the paper to the captain. "The only connection between all of them are run-down buildings, which brings everything back to O'Shannahan."

"Well, I would say you must've caused some concern for this creep since there hasn't been any more activity."

"That's a good thing, but I feel like I'm running out of time. This perp may be laying low at the moment, but at some point, they're going to get someone else. I don't like not being ahead of them."

"I agree." The captain huffed. "I know you're doing your best, and we just don't have much manpower to help you out. Be careful with O'Shannahan though, he can ruin your career, and I don't want to see that happen. Be absolutely sure he's involved before you go after him."

Dawson sighed. "I know, which is why we're sitting here in limbo…because I have nothing concrete. If I could just get in Finn's building. In my gut, there's a clue there, but he won't cooperate, and I have no evidence or probable cause to get a warrant."

"I'll talk to him and see if we can get him to open it up for us. It's empty and has been for a long time. I'll keep you posted."

"Thanks. I appreciate it." Dawson returned to his thoughts after the captain left the room. If he could smooth the waters with O'Shannahan, maybe he'd get his break after all. The more time that passed, the greater the odds that the killer would strike again before they solved this.

Dawson grabbed his keys and decided to head back over to the original crime scene and the diner. There had to be something they were missing, although with all the rain that had come and gone since the killings, there probably wasn't much left of the scene. The crime-scene tape had been torn in half at the alley. No doubt the homeless needed to get back to their space. Forensics had been done with the scene and processed everything they found, but Dawson wanted to see what he could find without the evidence being right in front of him.

The blood still stained the ground and had not completely washed away. Dawson wandered around it and looked at the ground from all angles before turning his attention to the wall. Faint blood splatter remained there, too. He pulled out a tape measure and measured the distance from the ground to the blood splatter. His guess was this person wasn't overly tall, maybe five-six or seven, give or take an inch or two. That didn't give them a lot to go on, but as he put the tape measure away, he turned toward the dumpster that was close by. It was full, and the stench that came from it indicated it hadn't been emptied in a while.

He went to the side of it and tried to move it a bit to look behind it. It was too full to even budge the damn thing, and he swore under his breath. It was reinventing the wheel to go through this all again. Every piece of likely evidence had been picked up and nothing helpful had come back. Even fingerprints were too plentiful, and with the amount of homeless people around, there was no way to get a hit on any of them.

He moved back to the street and looked at the diner. The front door was still taped up. He walked around to the alley behind it and went through the same process of looking at the site of the body from every angle. He sat down on the crates still stacked there. Even the cigarette butts remained littered on the ground. The back door wasn't taped off, so he tried the door and it opened.

He slipped under the crime scene tape and entered the kitchen of the diner. The spoiled meat had been thrown out, and the counters cleaned of the mess. At least the flies were gone, now that there was no food lying out.

Nothing in the kitchen indicated a struggle had happened in here. Dawson went into the dining room and sat at the counter, facing the tables. He tried to envision the patrons in there: Eugene getting his free meal with his benefactor, Darla pushing her business, Amy mingling with the customers and bringing smiles, and even Beth, being ridiculed and hating her job. Amy wasn't a tall girl, but about average height. Beth was smaller, maybe five-three. Neither looked like they could have enough strength to mutilate someone's face, even if they were in a rage.

Darla's ex had been cleared. He may not have had a solid alibi, but he didn't have motive either. He was doing his job and trying to stay out of trouble, especially being on probation. Dawson had talked to his PO, and the man had said he hadn't seen anyone more determined to get his life straight. Darla was linked to Finn, just as Eugene was, but Charlie wasn't...at least not that Dawson could see. Which took him right back to the dead end.

He stood up and made his way back through the kitchen and went outside. He closed the door and sighed. There was nothing that could be found. He'd gone over the evidence again and again. Nothing. Disgust and frustration oozed from him.

His phone beeped with a text. Captain Collins.

Got permission. Meet me at the building.

Dawson's lips curled into a smile. Damn, he actually did it. He had no doubt Mr. O'Shannahan would be there bitching the whole time they were searching. He headed to the building to await the captain and the owner.

Dawson arrived before the others and waited in his car. Five minutes, ten minutes passed. As the time ticked past the thirty-minute mark, he was getting anxious. He got out of the car and walked across the street to the front of the building. The door had been slightly open before. Today, a padlock was keeping it shut. About that time, the captain drove up with Finn O'Shannahan right behind him, as well as two other squad cars and Officer Brown in a separate vehicle. It was quite the spectacle seeing all of them drive up in a row.

Finn scowled as he walked up to Dawson. "I didn't do this for you."

Dawson nodded. "I appreciate it just the same, sir."

Finn grunted and unlocked the door, then stood back as they walked by him. Flashlights in hand, they entered the building. Three of the officers went to the second floor, and Dawson and Brown stayed on the main level with Captain Collins and Finn O'Shannahan.

Sweeping the lights down the hall, they came to the first door. Dawson stood back as Finn came forward to unlock it. Once Finn stepped aside to allow Dawson to pass, he walked into a small living room. A dilapidated couch was against the wall. Wallpaper was peeling off the walls and the stench was overwhelming.

Dawson covered his mouth with a bandana and continued into the next room. A full-size bed was against the far wall, with an armoire on another. Walls were grimy, but nothing in the room other than those two pieces of furniture.

The bathroom and kitchen yielded the same. Nothing. They moved back into the hallway and continued to the next locked door. Again, a near-empty apartment with no clues. Grime covered the walls. Cockroaches scattered as the flashlight beam hit them, sending them scurrying for a dark place. Dawson cringed. He guessed these places hadn't had a person in them in decades.

As they came to the final door on the main hallway, Finn came forward with his set of keys. After trying all of them, he finally managed to get it open.

Dawson and Brown pushed into the room. It was small—not a full apartment like the others. A tiny cot was against one wall, with an insignificant round table on another. A candle and black crayon were on the table. A door near the table stood ajar. Dawson pulled it open to find an empty closet.

He leaned forward with his hands on the partition. "Damn it," he muttered. "There has to be something here."

He wanted to bang his head against the back of the closet in frustration, but hearing Finn speak with the captain about knowing they wouldn't find anything, he stood straight up and shut the door.

The other three officers who'd gone to the second floor returned with the report that it was empty and no signs of inhabitants for years, just like on the main floor.

Dawson turned and held his hand out to Finn. "Thank you, sir, for allowing the search. I appreciate your help in this matter."

Finn looked down at Dawson's hand, and for a second, Dawson thought he would refuse the handshake. With a sigh, Finn finally shook it. "I told you from the beginning I had nothing to hide and was not involved."

Dawson nodded. "Just needed to be thorough, sir."

Finn silently bobbed his head. Once everyone passed by him, he locked the doors again.

"When did you say this was scheduled for demolition?" Dawson asked.

"Should have been done by now, but it was postponed due to zoning issues for the new project. I don't have a timetable yet."

Dawson stared at the building. There was something about that room. It didn't feel right, but he couldn't put his finger on it...not yet.

thirty-one

I held my breath. That was too close for comfort. I clutched the list and the hatchet. I'd heard the voices in the hall and had grabbed everything that would incriminate me, then slid into the hidden room at the back of the closet. No one knew it was there. I'd found it quite by accident one day when I was exploring the building. It was perfect for just these moments.

The detective was frustrated. I could hear it in his voice. I'd been listening at the hidden panel when he'd entered the closet. His breathing was heavy. I'd been holding my breath, scared to death he would find me.

I looked down at the hatchet in my hand. It was so familiar in my grasp now. I hardly felt the weight and longed for the feel of the adrenaline kicking in when the blade made its first cut into a face; the feel of the warm blood spurting over me as I brought the hatchet up for another blow. I don't think the sensation of power would ever get old. The list contained four names plus my first guinea-pig victim, and yet, I wanted more.

As I slid the panel open and put the hatchet and list back on the table, the pain in my head hit hard. I grabbed the wall to keep myself upright as blackness swirled in front of my eyes. Voices calling out in my mind began softly and became louder and louder. The mantra, "Father, don't make me do it," came faster and faster the louder it got.

Emma, I did it to save us.

With that thought, I collapsed to the floor.

Dawson glanced down at his watch. 5:00 p.m. He had just enough time to run home and shower before picking up Ali for dinner. After the hot shower, he dressed in record time in jeans and a light blue oxford shirt. As comfortable as things were between him and Ali, he couldn't help but feel a bit anxious as he headed for the door.

Flipping lights off behind him, he reached the front door in the dark. Just as he reached for the outside light to turn on before he left, a shadow moved across his driveway. He strained his eyes, trying to make out who or what it was. The height made it a who, but it was too dark to see anything. He flipped on the outside light and opened the door, but he or she had vanished into the shadows.

He locked the door and moved cautiously to his car, his eyes taking in every shadow on the edge of the driveway. He turned toward the empty house across the street. Lights were on in the front part of the home, which he knew came on with a timer. No sign of any other life. With a shrug, he returned to the driver's side, got in the car, and glanced at his watch. He sent off a text to Ali letting her know he was on his way, but would be a couple of minutes late.

Regardless, he made good time driving from his place to hers. His stomach knotted as he rang her doorbell. He felt like a teenager all over again. When she opened the door, he was tongue-tied. The jade-colored dress that hugged her figure had him speechless.

"Is this alright?" she asked quietly.

"Yes. You're beautiful."

"Thank you. You clean up pretty good yourself." She grabbed her purse and locked the door. "Ready?"

He walked her around to the passenger side, and opened the door for her. He was quiet as he got into the car and started to The Log Cabin.

"You're quiet tonight. What's on your mind?" Ali's voice broke into his thoughts.

"Just the case, I guess." He sighed and gave her a quick glance. "O'Shannahan gave us permission to search the building. Dead end."

"You're not really surprised by that, are you?"

"Yes, and no. I was hoping for some sort of a lead. There must be a connection to that building. Why else is it on the list?"

She laid a hand on his arm. "We don't know what that list is really about. Can you tie it to anything else?"

He swore softly. "No. The three addresses don't seem to have any connection. Well, the diner was the third vics and the other address was Beth's parents. And she worked at the diner. This last address...abandoned. Nothing there."

Ali withdrew her hand, and he immediately felt the loss of her touch. "Maybe there is a connection, and you just haven't found it yet."

He nodded. "Maybe. I just feel like time's running out. If I don't find something soon, I fear there will be another victim and we'll be no closer to getting this lunatic than before."

"I understand that, but you can't overthink it. I know I'm telling the wind to stop blowing if I try to tell you not to think about it for the night." She took a breath. "But let's get through dinner without talking about it, enjoy ourselves, and then after we eat, we can run over things again if you want."

"Agreed. I'm sorry, Ali. I shouldn't have brought it up."

"There is no should or shouldn't, Wes. We know this business, and we both know that we're so engrossed in our jobs that it overlaps with our personal life. I get it. No apologies." She smiled. "It's one of the things I really like about you."

He grinned. "There's more than one?"

She shrugged noncommittally.

"That's all I get?"

She laughed. "That's all you deserve."

The rest of the drive to Clinton went quickly as Ali talked about her day. She kept the details to a minimum, which he appreciated greatly. They'd just fallen into a comfortable silence when he turned into the parking lot for The Log Cabin. Every space was nearly full, but they managed to find a spot not far from the building.

As they walked through the door, they were greeted with the hustle and bustle of a well-established restaurant. Tables were filled, and waitresses moved quickly throughout the dining room. The hostess welcomed them. "Reservation?"

"Dawson."

"Yes, for two. Right this way."

He gestured for Ali to move ahead of him and smiled as he admired her from the back. As she arrived at the table, he pulled out her chair for her.

"Thank you," she murmured as she slid into her seat.

The hostess left two menus on the table and quietly slipped off without a word.

Dawson surveyed the room, taking in the couples around them as well as the lights that were dimmed, but only enough to create a comfortable atmosphere, yet still bright enough to actually see.

"Anything suspicious?" Ali teased.

He met her gaze. "Just trying to keep you safe."

She rolled her eyes and laughed. "So chivalrous."

After ordering, and the waitress placing their drinks in front of them, Dawson sat back and just watched Ali. Her hair was not in its usual ponytail. It hung free around her shoulders and she'd curled it gently next to her face. She had the tiniest hint of makeup on.

He smiled when he realized that she was watching him in amusement at his perusal of her.

She leaned forward. "Like what you see?"

He reached across the table. As her warm hand rested in his, he whispered, "Absolutely, beautiful." A soft blush spread across her cheeks. "You are beautiful, Ali."

She raised her glass. "To a quiet, relaxing evening… one that is much needed and deserved by both of us."

He lifted his glass and clicked hers faintly. "Here, here."

They sat back as the food arrived. Ali's meal—a chicken and artichoke plate covered with a lemon sauce and served with a salad—smelled delicious. He almost wished he'd ordered the same, until his dinner was placed in front of him: a rib-eye steak and baked potato with broccoli. His mouth watered at the sight of the steak, medium-rare.

"That looks good." Ali pointed at his plate.

"As does yours."

He ate in silence as did Ali. His steak was so tender and he was enjoying a good meal, having eaten so much take-out lately. Ali appeared to be enjoying her own food as she ate with enthusiasm.

She sat back and pushed her plate away. "I'm stuffed. That was so good."

He grinned. "It must have been. You sure you don't want to lick it clean?" He gestured to her empty plate.

"I don't believe in wasting food." She feigned being insulted.

"Well, *I'm* not quite done. So, while I eat, tell me about your family. You know about mine."

She cocked her head slightly to the left as she watched him. "Not much to tell really. My parents were older when they had me. I felt most of the time like I was living with my grandparents. They were great and always so supportive, but I was a loner, mostly because they were older and I had no siblings. They died a few years back, about a year apart. Now it's just me. I tend to throw myself into my work...which you know. Other than that, that's my life in a nutshell."

"How was it to be an only child? You probably don't really know what you missed."

"Hmm." She pondered the question. "I guess you're right. I never really knew what I was missing. I'd see TV shows or movies with siblings and always craved that. They always seemed so close. I guess I missed just having someone to talk to—tell secrets to. You know, that kind of stuff."

"And I, at times, longed for a house where I was the only child. Maybe you just always want what you can't have."

"Probably, that is very true." She took a sip of water. "It's lonely though when you are an only child."

"It can be pretty lonely when you're surrounded by people."

The waitress appeared to take their empty plates. "Dessert?"

Dawson smiled at Ali. "Cheesecake?"

"I don't think I could eat another bite, but you go ahead."

He looked up at the waitress. "One white chocolate raspberry cheesecake, please...and two forks."

The waitress smiled knowingly and slipped away.

"I just said I was full."

"Yup, but if you haven't had this cheesecake, you've got to at least try it. And I guarantee once you do, you'll be eating more of it."

"Easy for you. You'll work it off, but I'm stuck behind a desk most of the time."

He smiled. "I'll help you work it off."

The words hung between them. He almost wished he could take them back, but he also wanted her response. She smiled and blushed, but didn't say a word.

The arrival of the cheesecake saved them from the moment becoming uncomfortable.

"Oh, my god that looks decadent," Ali gushed. She reached for the fork and took the first bite.

He watched as she closed her eyes and enjoyed the taste and creaminess of it. This was his favorite dessert, and to watch her show total bliss at the taste of it was almost too much for him to take in.

She opened her eyes and looked at him. "You better get some while you can."

"I knew it. Should I get you your own piece?"

"No. I really can't eat much more, but maybe one more bite."

He rolled his eyes. "You are a goner. Next time, I'm ordering your own regardless of how full you say you are."

"Next time, huh?" She batted her eyes at him as she reached for another forkful.

He'd been right. Ali had eaten at least half of the piece of cheesecake. He swore she'd eaten more than that, but she denied even eating half of it.

As they walked to the car, he kept an arm around her.

"Thank you," he whispered as he opened the door for her. "I haven't relaxed this much in a long time."

"My pleasure, Mr. Dawson."

The drive home was done in comfortable silence. Both seemingly lost in their own thoughts. What Ali was thinking, Dawson could only imagine. But he was trying to figure out how to wrangle an invite into her house when they got back. He didn't want the evening to end.

thirty-two

Dinner had been great. Ali had seen another side to Wes. A soft flirtatious side that came easy to him. She didn't want the night to end and although it was a comfortable silence on the drive home, she desperately hoped he'd want to stay with her tonight.

Her mind wandered to the cheesecake. The taste of it was orgasmic, but seeing him watch her as she slid every mouthful into her mouth was worth every calorie she consumed. She had purposely chosen this dress to see if she could push him to realize his feelings for her. Jade was a color she knew she could wear well, and the low-cut front gave her the reaction she'd wanted when she'd opened the door.

She was shameless in her attempt to have Wes see her for the woman she was, and not just a medical examiner and friend. She hoped her intuition was right. This couldn't continue the way it was…a longing on her part every time she saw him—touched him. It left her aching at night. No, tonight was the night it either all came together, or she'd put her feelings aside to stay the friends he wanted to be, knowing that if he made that choice, it would never change.

She swallowed nervously as he pulled up to her house. It was now or never.

Pulling into Ali's driveway, Dawson shut the engine off and turned to face her.

"I had a great time, Wes," she said quietly, shifting to lean toward him a little.

"I did, too."

"I should get going." She reached for the handle.

He got out and came around the car just as she was getting out.

He walked her to the door, suddenly having a case of the nerves again—damn teenage hormones flaring. She unlocked the door and turned to him. He thought for a moment she was going to say good night and slip into the house before he even had a chance to kiss her. She watched him for a moment, her eyes searching his.

"Do you want to come in?" she asked softly.

He nodded slightly. "Do you want me to?"

She didn't answer, just simply reached for his hand and led him inside.

Dawson shut the door behind them as they entered the house. He looked around as he followed Ali into the main room, an open-concept living room-kitchen area. She turned toward him, and he let his gaze wander down her body, taking in the dress hugging every curve, then back up to meet her eyes.

He stepped closer and pulled her to him. Her sandalwood perfume was not overpowering, but it was intoxicating, drawing him further in. His lips easily found hers as he tried to hold back the overwhelming desire for her.

She sighed softly and pressed against him. He swung her around and pushed her against the wall, deepening their kiss. His need for her surged. He held her wrists and lifted her arms above her head. He pushed his hips into her body, pinning her to the wall, then pulled back from the kiss to look at her. Her eyes were closed, her breathing heavy.

Did she have any idea the effect her desirability had on him?

He lowered his head to nibble the side of her neck, then stopped at her shoulder. He let go of her hands and took a step back. Her eyes opened quickly, questioning him.

With a sly smile, he reached for the side zipper of her dress, but she brushed his hand aside and unzipped it herself. It slid from her shoulders and fell in a pool of fabric around her ankles.

Dawson exhaled slowly as she stood before him in just her bra and black-lace panties. He hardened at the vision of her. She met his eyes, and slowly reached behind herself and unhooked her bra. He watched—heart pounding—as it dropped to the floor.

He reached for her, settling his hands at her waist, and as he lifted her, her legs wrapped around him. She tenderly caressed the back of his neck, then plunged her hands into his hair as he captured her nipple in his mouth and teased her with his tongue. Her moan was all the encouragement he needed as he nipped lightly, wanting to prolong the moment.

She let out a strangled whisper, "down the hall to the right," and he turned and headed for the bedroom, letting her guide him as he continued his heated assault on her breasts. He eagerly carried her and ignored the fact that the journey down the hall seemed too long, when in essence it was only a few steps to the doorway.

She flipped on the light as he stepped inside the bedroom. He crossed to the bed and lowered her down slowly. She watched him as he stripped away his clothes, his body reacting to her gaze. Now fully naked, he reached for her last piece of clothing—that sexy black lace thong—and pulled it off.

He looked down at her perfect body and slowly slid his hands up her thighs and all the way to her hips. He knelt between her legs and continued his gentle caress, exploring every inch of her.

Ali sighed and closed her eyes, enjoyment showing on her face.

He lowered himself on top of her, and she moved her hips to greet him as he slid into the slick opening. It felt so right…like he was finally home.

Weeks, days, whatever it was, he could only think that the buildup to this moment had pushed him to the brink. The feel of her beneath him was his undoing. They moved in frantic time, unable to get enough of each other.

She dug her nails into his back and whimpered as she climaxed, pushing him over the edge. He made a motion to move off her, but she tightened her legs around him, keeping him in place.

He kissed her softly before whispering, "so much for that not happening."

thirty-three

Dawson awoke with the ring of his phone. He was curled around Ali and swore softly as he turned away from her. Reaching for his jeans and searching the pockets for his phone, he found it just as it went to voicemail. Looking at the caller ID, he saw Brown's number.

"Damn it." Dawson slid from under the covers and started getting dressed.

"Trouble?" Ali's voice was muffled as she buried her head in the pillow.

"I don't know. Missed a call from the precinct." He glanced at his watch. "5:00 a.m. Something must be going on."

She rolled over, but he noticed how she kept her eyes on him as he put his shirt on. "Go," she said. "It's your job. I get it."

He sat down on the edge of the bed. How could someone look so beautiful just waking up? Her hair was disheveled, but at the same time, sexy as all hell. He leaned over and kissed her gently on the lips. "I know you understand, but you make it very difficult to walk out that door."

She sat up—keeping the sheet covering herself—snaked a free arm around his neck, and pulled him close for another kiss. "Now get to work and keep me posted. I'll be headed to the office as soon as I shower."

He groaned. "I'd rather shower with you."

She laughed. "Get out. Go do your job."

"Killjoy," he mumbled under his breath as he left the room. A moment later, he shut the door, signaling his departure.

He'd no sooner backed out of Ali's driveway when his phone rang again. "Dawson."

"Sir, Mrs. O'Shannahan is at the station. She's asking for you. Insisting on talking to you immediately."

"On my way. I'll be there in ten." Dawson hung up without another word. Katie asking for him at the precinct was not a good sign, and the closer he got, the bigger the knot in his stomach grew. He'd been fearing this moment would come.

He entered the police station and headed immediately to the bullpen. Brown stopped him before he got there. "Room One."

"Why is she in there?" Dawson asked over his shoulder.

Brown kept on his heels. "She insisted. Sir?"

Dawson stopped at the tone in the young officer's voice. "What is it?"

"She won't talk to anyone but you. But sir, it's not pretty."

Dawson nodded and took a breath before opening the door. The sight before him when he entered was the view of Katie's back as she was sitting faced away from the door. He moved slowly around the table. "Katie?"

She looked up as he sat down across from her. Her right eye was swollen shut and bruising had already purpled around it. It looked like the right side of her face had taken the force as the mark went from her eye to her chin. She kept her eyes averted and stared at her own hands folded on the table.

"What happened?" he asked softly.

"I fell into the wall."

"Bullshit. Why are you here if you aren't going to tell the truth?" He slammed his hands down on the table, angry at Katie for hiding what was happening and mad at himself for having no control of this conversation.

"Detective Dawson, you don't understand."

"I understand more than you think, Katie. Who did this to you?"

She shook her head. "A news reporter showed up at the house and started asking about the killings and if Finn was still under suspicion."

Dawson sat back, waiting.

"Finn was angry. He blames me for the press being there and—"

"Why does he blame you?"

She smiled cunningly. "You and I both know why, detective. And he's right. I leaked the story that he was being questioned. I thought he might have been kept longer. I almost prayed that he was guilty."

"Do you think he's involved at all in these murders?"

She shook her head. "No. But I wanted to blame him for my father. Dad never would've died if Finn hadn't displaced him from his home."

"So, what happened to you?"

She stood and paced the small room. "Finn was furious with the press. It doesn't matter. I guess I came just to see if you have any news about Dad's killer?"

"Did this happen this morning or last night?"

She shrugged. "I fell into the wall last night."

Dawson sighed. "Do you want to file charges?"

She hesitated and he thought for a moment she was going to say yes. Instead, she shook her head slowly. "I don't think there's anything you can do to prosecute the wall."

Dawson's phone beeped with a text. *My office, now.*

"Excuse me for a moment. I'm going to send in Officer Brown in case you decide to name *that wall*. I'll be back to check on you." He paused. "Will you be okay?" he asked softly.

She nodded. "Yes. You don't need to hold my hand. I just wanted to talk to you first. You have a way of putting one's anxiety at ease."

He walked out of the room. Katie played the victim well, but then showed strength and a hint of manipulation. He couldn't read her. Was she playing him?

He made his way to the captain's office. "Sir?"

"What is she doing here? You know after O'Shannahan agreed for us to search the building, I assumed we wouldn't have any more issues with him."

"Did you see her face? Is he immune to the law?" Dawson's anger made it hard to rein in his disgust with the captain. This was a local matter, he knew that. His job was to work the murders, not get involved with domestic violence cases.

"Not your case, Dawson. Do your job and stop causing other issues in my precinct. Besides, I understand she isn't saying she was hit by Finn."

Dawson sighed. "I had nothing to do with this. I offered her a chance to talk earlier when I knew something was going on. She finally had enough and came in. Brown is tending to it." He stood, moved to the door, and turned back to the captain. "Trust me, sir, I want these murders solved as quickly as you do."

Dawson returned to the conference room with the victimology board. He stared at it, taking in the map where there were colored pins to indicate deaths and addresses that he'd been left. In his gut, he knew there was something more to that building they'd searched yesterday, but he couldn't put his finger on it. He'd been sure they'd find some sort of clue there.

thirty-four

I have no idea how long I had laid passed out on the floor. My head was throbbing as I came to, and I sat up cautiously. These headaches were getting worse. I closed my eyes, sitting there, trying to remember what had happened. *Emma, I did it for us* had run through my mind. Who was Emma? I saw a flash of red and the tip of an ax. It didn't look the hatchet I'd been using. Was my mind playing tricks on me?

I stood warily. The wooziness was gone, but the headache prevailed. The detective. He'd been in this room. I needed to move forward quicker with my plan. I could feel the heat of him closing in, and I had to finish the list. I had to extract the revenge I'd been planning for years.

I picked up the list and looked at the last two names. It wouldn't take long for him to figure out the connection, once I finished with the last victim.

My mind flashed to my first victim, the homeless man—the killing that had given me confidence and proved I could do this. Maybe another random body would be just the dead-end trail the detective would follow and allow me some breathing space. I'd wait until tonight, and then I'd find that person. Maybe I could kill someone who'd hit a little closer to home for Mr. Arrogant Detective. My mouth curled into a smile. Who could I target that would hurt him the most?

He'd gotten quite close with that medical examiner, but she'd be hard to get to. Tonight, would not be the night to strike. I needed to watch him and find his most vulnerable spot. In the meantime, I couldn't risk anything being found.

I took the list and the hatchet and placed them in the hidden room…just in case the detective decided to return.

I slid the paneled wall back into place. I'd found this gem of a hideout by accident when I first stumbled into this abandoned building. I'd been running, looking for a place to hide ten years ago. At that time, the front door was unlocked even though no one lived here. The place had been abandoned for quite some time. The first two doors in the long hallway were locked, but this room had been unlocked. There wasn't much in it. No sink, no bathroom. It was a hidden space that simply had a cot and a table. At one time, I envisioned it being a servant's quarters before this had been converted to apartments.

In its heyday, this building must have been something. Being in what used to be an upper-class neighborhood, it had originally been the only house on the street. Over the years, more buildings had cropped up, and this one was converted to apartments and eventually run down with only the low of the low renting it. Drug dealers and unemployed people squatted here for years before it was condemned, and somehow, they managed to clear everyone out. No one had returned.

It was my lucky day when I walked through that door.

The room was in shambles, and sure, there was no running water or even a bathroom, but it served my purpose as a hideout. I knew I wouldn't be living there full time, and in fact, I'd kept nothing here until recently. Then the hatchet had found its home here, and my cloak, unless I was cleaning it. I kept a box of garbage bags in the hidden room for the purpose of carrying the cloak home to wash it.

The mystery room. My other accidental find. I thought I'd heard something and jumped into the closet to hide. I'd pressed against the back wall, trying to make myself as small as possible and felt the wall give. The paneling hadn't been put in place properly, and I was able to pull it open. Stepping inside the small space was like stepping back in time. It was empty, but it held a feeling of being safe. I closed the paneling from the inside. A moment of panic hit me when I thought I might not be able to get out. I could die in there, and no one would even know I was gone.

It had been easy to open from the inside though, and I found myself excited. There could be so many uses for this room. It was the very place I made my plan and my list of people who needed to be severed from my life.

Severed.

It was a strange word. It reminded me of cutting, hence the hatchet came into play. I'd played with the idea of a knife, but ax kept creeping into my mind like a memory. One I couldn't place. As I began looking at axes, I realized it would be heavy and hard to conceal. That's when I found the camping ax, or hatchet. It was smaller, easily concealed in my cloak.

The plan had formed, and somehow, I was driven by thoughts that felt like I had had them before. A memory, with no recollection as to why. It wasn't until after the first kill that the headaches started, along with flashes. They were small at first, but suddenly with every kill, they became stronger. The voices then started. A conversation between me and someone else; at least I thought it was me. I couldn't remember the conversation, but it was like a movie that played through my mind. I didn't recognize any of the characters, and yet, I felt I was a part of it.

I'd been pacing the hidden room one day when I felt a small draft on the back wall. I searched and searched and couldn't find anything, yet the wall was cold. It had to be an outside wall, but where was the draft coming from?

It had taken me weeks, but I finally found the nail in the wall that stuck out just a bit. It had been undetectable until I ran my hand over it. Pressing on it opened a small half door that led to the outside back alley. I had made sure the inside door was unlocked in case I couldn't figure out how to get the outside door open. The inside of the door was wooden and blended right into the wall. The outside was brick and was undetectable in the alley as a door.

Outside I searched and searched the bricks for something that would open it from the outside. I finally found a small corner of a brick that stuck out a fraction. Pushing on it opened the small door. Sometimes, I used the front door in and out, but after the second killing, I decided to use the back entrance and keep the main door locked at all times. At some point, someone had come and put a padlock on the front door of the building. I was undeterred and started using the secret entrance. There was no way anyone would find me. But now the detective had been inside my room, and I was once again feeling violated.

Time to hurt him where it counts.

thirty-five

Dawson made his way across the street to Ali's office. He had so much to do, but after leaving in a hurry that morning and still in the clothes he wore last night, he needed to make sure she wasn't feeling slighted. He'd never been that guy who snuck out after sex, or to leave in the morning while his partner was still in bed. Guilt flooded him as he walked down the sterile hall to her office.

She was bent over her desk writing furiously with stacks of files in front of her. Her hair was, once again, pulled back in the familiar ponytail. He cleared his throat, and she looked up.

"Hey. Everything okay?" She moved the files on the chair and motioned for him to sit.

"Yeah, I guess. Typical police stuff." He studied her. Her work persona was definitely different than that of the woman he'd held in his arms last night. "I just wanted to check in with you. I'm sorry about leaving like I did."

"Nothing to be sorry about. It's the nature of your job." She smiled. "Did you think I'd be upset?"

"Honestly, I wasn't sure."

She leaned forward in her chair, her arms resting on her desk. "I'm a big girl, Wes. I can handle you being called into work."

He smiled. "Good. Because trust me, leaving you this morning was not what I wanted to be doing at 5:00 a.m."

"I didn't think you were trying to escape, if that's what you were worried about." She leaned back. "I did, however, wonder if there had been another killing."

He shook his head. "Not yet, but I feel like it's been quiet for a few days and this isn't over. I'm headed to City Hall to see if I can get the blueprints for that abandoned building."

"I thought nothing was there?"

"There wasn't anything. But my gut tells me that building has something to do with the murders. I need to see what the original plans were. Maybe we missed something. A way to the basement or something." He sighed. "And the captain is breathing down my neck again. He definitely isn't happy that the state police are in his house."

"Collins is all bark. Don't let him get to you."

Dawson rolled his eyes. "Easier said than done." He stood and hesitated a minute. "I'll text you later?"

"I hope so." She smiled. Her phone rang, giving him the chance to escape without having to decide on whether he should kiss her or not. She raised her hand in a wave as she reached for the phone.

Dawson approached City Hall. He had no idea what it was he was truly searching for, but he hoped he'd know when he came across it. He'd felt something in that building, in the small room. A heaviness that just reminded him of evil. He couldn't pinpoint it, but it was heaviest in the small room. He needed to know when the house was built and who originally lived there. At this point, he wouldn't be at all surprised if some relative of Lizzie Borden owned it. And once again, he was chasing ghosts.

The planning board told him the blueprints were archived and would take a couple of days to get. He filled out the necessary paperwork.

"We'll give you a call when they are ready."

"Please rush this. It's police business." The young girl behind the desk didn't look too impressed with the request.

He left City Hall and drove back to the building. Sitting outside, he took in every window and door he could see on the front of the house. There was a small alley that ran along one side of it.

He strolled down the alley and found a dead end at the back of the house. More windows, but no door on the back side. This sparked a stirring in him. Fire code would require a second door. The alley dead-ended behind this particular building, but ran down the back of the other houses to the left. Dawson went as far as he could before the alley dead-ended into a wall coming from the rear of the house. He'd have to go around the other side. The back of the building had a brick finish on the first floor. The second floor had old shake siding, which was falling off in various sections.

He strode around to the front of the building and started to go to the other side when his phone rang.

"Dawson."

"I will have your job," the deep voice snarled.

"Excuse me? Who is this?"

"Just stay away from me. I'll have your neck on the chopping block."

Before Dawson could reply the call was ended. Finn O'Shannahan. He couldn't prove it, as the number had been blocked from caller ID, but who else would threaten his job? And on the heels of his wife sporting a black eye?

He jogged across the street to his car. He needed to check on Katie's status.

He arrived to find the large man ranting at Collins inside the station. Collins was listening to Finn, but anyone could tell he was holding back. Dawson slipped past without being seen and went to the room where Katie had been. She was gone.

"Brown?"

"Sir, conference room." Brown didn't even look up.

Dawson turned on his heel and made his way to the conference room next door to where all the investigation for the murders was set up. Katie sat at the table, sipping a diet soda. She startled when he opened the door.

"Finn is here to pick me up, isn't he?" she asked calmly.

"Do you *want* him to pick you up?" Dawson demanded, trying to keep the frustration from his voice.

"Not really. I don't want to see him right now. I asked the nice young man if I could wait here a bit. I don't know if I should. Finn will be really angry and I don't think you can keep him from bringing me home." Her voice was fast with fear.

"We can't do anything until you tell us who gave you that shiner, Katie. Finish the report with Officer Brown, please." Dawson moved to the door to call for Brown when he heard Finn's voice.

"Where is my wife?" The window in the door was frosted so Dawson knew he couldn't see into the room, but he gestured for Katie to move to the side of the wall away from the door. "Collins, hand her over."

"I'm not holding your wife, sir." The captain's voice was strained and Dawson knew it was only a matter of time before the captain would probably give Katie up to save face with the politician. The joys of being an elected official.

Dawson looked over his shoulder. Katie stood back against the wall, wringing her hands. The purple bruise stood out against the whiteness of her face.

The voices moved on down the hallway and Dawson opened the door just enough to slip out. He found Brown, and with a murmur, directed him to go finish the report and get the charges filed. He didn't want O'Shannahan to leave the station. Brown hurried to the conference room and Dawson stood there waiting until the door shut behind the officer. He heard the voices returning to the area and Dawson started for the front door.

"Dawson!" The bellow stopped him in his tracks. Turning slowly, he faced Finn. The man seemed larger than he did before, his hands clenched at his sides. "Where's my wife?"

"I have no idea." Dawson kept his voice neutral and glanced at the captain, who shook his head, giving no indication of what he was thinking.

"Mr. O'Shannahan," the captain said, "I told you, she's not here. Maybe you should go home. She may have returned by now." The captain danced around the politically correct thing to do, lying blatantly to the man.

"I'll have *both* your jobs." Finn pointed at Dawson and then to the captain. "You can't keep me from my wife."

"Why would you think she's here, sir?" Dawson broke in. "Did she have a problem that required the police?" He knew he was baiting him, but he couldn't resist.

The man plowed passed Dawson. "She better not be here," was the only response Dawson heard as he was pushed to the wall. He started to speak, but he stopped when Collins' hand went up to silence him.

Collins watched the man leave the building, then turned to Dawson. "Stay to the murder investigation. I don't want to see you go in that room again where Mrs. O'Shannahan is. Understand?"

"Yes, sir, unless it ties that man back to the murders." Dawson tried to hold back the grin, but he knew this situation was becoming more and more dangerous. As soon as Katie was ready, they needed to find her a safe place where Finn wouldn't be able to get to her. And, the captain was right. He had to stay out of it, no matter if he was the only one Katie trusted.

She exited the conference room hours later. Dawson had been pacing the room next door, trying to work on theories and find new clues, but his mind was elsewhere. He heard Brown asking her if she had a safe place to go. She was walking out the police station door when Dawson caught up with her.

"Hey, do you have somewhere to go?"

Katie turned and looked at him. "I called my friend, Jenna. She said I could stay there." Her eyes held defeat.

"I'll take you." Dawson glanced around. The streets were empty.

She started to protest, but he was insistent. This was the least he could do, knowing that part of the reason this had happened was because he'd pushed Finn on the questioning and searching of the building. He, no doubt, had taken it out on Katie even if she wouldn't name him.

"She only lives a couple of blocks away," Katie whispered. Her quiet tone was mouse-like, yet her posture spoke of confidence and not at all like a woman running from an abuser.

"I'm driving. Come on." He directed her to his car.

Arriving at her friend's, Dawson walked her to the door. "Are you sure you're okay here?"

Katie nodded. "Jenna and I have known each other for years, even if lately we haven't been as close as we once were. I trust her."

The door opened and a tall brunette stood before him. She took one look at Katie and pulled her into a hug. "You're staying here as long as you like." She turned her head toward him. "I'm Jenna."

"I'm Detective Dawson. I just wanted to make sure she got here safe. Here's my card, if you need anything. Call day or night." He handed her his business card, then put his attention on Katie. "Get some rest. I'll check in on you tomorrow."

Katie smiled faintly. "Thank you, Detective Dawson

Dawson made his way back to his car. He prayed she'd be safe here. His gut was screaming this was all tied to the murders, yet was that just the stress of the case and trying to find links when there really wasn't any? He couldn't face Collins again today, so he headed for home.

thirty-six

The man was stupid. I'd followed his car as he took the woman to a small cottage a few blocks away, closer to the tracks. I thought he'd been sidling up to that pretty medical examiner, but instead he was here with the high-falutin politician's wife.

I'd managed to stay unseen while he dropped off the woman. My spirits lifted further as the detective left. My fingers itched for the feel of the hatchet in my hand, and I knew I'd be back here later.

I made my way across town to my room. It was a bit far, but luckily, I had the car. I parked it a couple of blocks away. There was a short distance where I would be on the sidewalk instead of in the alleys. At night I didn't mind, but during the day, I felt exposed. Not that many people were around this run-down part of town much. I moved as quickly as I could to the building, without drawing attention to myself. Slipping around back, I checked my surroundings. Within seconds, I pushed the brick and slipped into the hidden room.

I inhaled deeply, exhaling my relief of being back in my safe place. I'd been here earlier in preparation, and the cloak hung in the closet. My hatchet propped against the wall. I picked it up and lovingly stroked the blade. My mind flashed images of pigeons and sudden blood splatter. I dropped the hatchet and fell against the wood.

Not again. I couldn't go through this again. I screamed and slid to the floor. The memories assaulted me in bits and pieces. Nothing fluid that I could tell where it was coming from. I didn't remember any of these pictures. Where were there pigeons in a roost, or a young woman with reddish-brown hair named Emma? I don't even know an Emma. The pounding in my head started again, and I was forced to close my eyes to try and control it.

These episodes had come more and more frequently, especially when I was holding the hatchet. It was a trigger of some sort, but I have no idea to what. I found myself lying down on the floor in the hidden room; one hand on the hatchet and the other cradling my head. I closed my eyes and drifted off to sleep with images flitting through my mind of a young girl laughing.

I have no idea how long I'd been sleeping. It was pitch dark in the room. I glanced at my watch. 10:30 pm. Close to the witching hour. I stood cautiously, but was relieved to find that the headache was gone. The adrenaline kicked in as I thought about my upcoming victim, and I changed quickly into my all-black outfit and cloak. I reached for the gloves and put them on. Picking up the hatchet, I slid it under the cloak.

I made my way back to my car, then drove the distance to the cottage. The lights were off. I crept forward in the cover of the shadows, keeping vigilant of everything around me. I circled the house, looking into windows, until I came to a room where the other woman was sleeping. The politician's wife was on the couch.

A sliding door at the back of the house led directly to

the living room. I pulled the hatchet free from the cloak and took a step toward the door. I yanked on it slightly. It was locked. I needed to find another way in.

I crept around the corner of the house and came to a door. Peering through the window, I saw a laundry room. The door was old. I tried turning knob, but it was also locked. I reached for my pocket and pulled out my driver's license. Sliding the card between the frame and the lock, I felt the door give. I pushed the door slowly open and stepped into the room. My heart pumped hard as my adrenaline kicked in, but I kept my senses and left the door ajar behind me for a quick getaway.

As I stood at the entrance to the living room, I saw empty wine glasses on the coffee table as well as a depleted bottle. With any luck, both of them had drunk enough to not wake easily. I crept softly toward the couch with my arm raised and the hatchet ready to strike.

I glanced at my watch. The clock ticked to 11:00. I swung my arm down, bringing the first blow right across her eyes. I rained ten more blows, crisscrossing each one over her face. At the end of the eleven, she was unrecognizable, just like her father. Eleven blows, eleven o'clock.

I smiled as the blood ran in trickles down her now-undecipherable cheeks onto the couch. A feeling of dread rolled over me. I hadn't enjoyed this kill like the others. I'd hardly felt the blood splatter as it hit me. A sense of loss struck at the realization that this kill meant nothing to me, and therefore, the joy wasn't there.

I stared down at the woman.

It was necessary. Wrong place, wrong time. If only you hadn't been so close to the cop.

The words ran through my mind as I took stock of how much blood was on me, and if I could maneuver from the house without leaving traces. My shoes hardly had any blood on them. I hadn't hit this one nearly as hard as some of the others I'd been so angry with.

With a sigh, I turned toward the door and ran from the scene.

Once my car was parked, I walked slower than normal through the shadows and alleys to my room. The headache was back, and for the first time since I'd started wielding the hatchet, I felt torn. Maybe a hint of remorse for what I'd done. But I also knew I'd just bought myself some more time to finish my list. Then I could disappear forever, and no one would even know the difference.

thirty-seven

Dawson had finally arrived home. After jumping in the shower, he put on fresh clothes, then donned his baseball cap and hoodie.

He'd driven by Finn's place a couple of times before making the trek home. The man's house had been dark and no vehicle was out front. Finn obviously wasn't home, and Dawson had no idea where to find him. So, in frustration, he'd turned his car toward home.

Now, he was headed for the streets again. Sara was close by—he knew it—and he needed her to be safe. Every day that passed without another killing was a blessing, but the unsolved crimes were hanging over him and the pressure was mounting to get the cases closed.

His phone vibrated with a text, and he ignored it. *Ali, please understand.* He trusted that on some level she *would* understand, but on the other hand, last night had elevated their relationship to a whole new level and now he was MIA. He'd been so preoccupied the rest of the day with Katie, and now, he wanted to get in his nightly search for Sara, which he hadn't done last night because of Ali and their date.

He started for a different section of town. The one where Finn's building stood. He hadn't looked for Sara in that neighborhood, but there were alleys in that area and abandoned houses. The perfect place to hide out if you didn't want to be found.

He slipped into the alley and knowing the dead end was to his right, he turned left behind the row of buildings. There weren't nearly as many homeless people here, in fact, it was very desolate. No people, no stench of human waste. He walked until he reached the end of the alley. Not one person had he found.

He'd seen the inside of Finn's building and there were no signs of even squatters being there. Dawson decided to walk up the sidewalk back to where he'd left his vehicle. It was the lone car on the street. This end of the city had really fallen into disrepair. It wasn't nearly as bad as the other side of the tracks, but needless to say, this city was losing its charm fast these days. The median income was becoming lower, since anyone with a drive to make money was moving to the better areas in the state, or even out of state altogether. Leighton was becoming a ghost town.

He laughed to himself. *A ghost town.* And he was chasing the ghost of Lizzie Borden, who apparently was staying two steps ahead of him all the way.

He pulled in his driveway to find Ali's car. She was sitting in it, reading a book. As he shut his vehicle off, she opened her door and got out.

"Hey, I just wanted to check to make sure you were okay. I heard about Katie." Ali stood near her car, not making any move to come closer.

Dawson, feeling like a heel, went around and leaned on his car facing her. "I'm okay. Just exhausted."

"Out looking for Sara?"

He nodded. "Nothing of course." He shrugged like it was no big deal, but he could feel his façade crumbling. He needed a break in some area of his life.

"I won't keep you. I was just worried." She turned toward her driver's door.

He reached out and grabbed her arm, then pulled her toward him as he closed the remaining space between them. "Don't go, please." His hands rested loosely on her hips, ready to let go if she chose to leave.

"I don't want to interfere with your night, Wes, but I was concerned. I know the stress you've been under."

He kissed her gently. "You're not interfering. I'd like you to stay." She pressed herself against him, holding him close. He nuzzled her neck, allowing himself to gather strength from her.

As they walked to the door, he looked over his shoulder and slowed. He pressed his key into Ali's hand. "Go ahead, I'll be right there," he whispered. He stood still, waiting until she was inside. He then turned and walked to the shadows of his driveway.

"Sara." He waited. Nothing. "Sara, please come out." Silence followed, and he stood there for what seemed like ages. "I miss you so much, Sara. Please don't leave a note and not talk to me." He waited for another few minutes and turned back to the house.

The hair on the back of his neck stood up; he knew he was being watched. He forced himself not to look back.

Ali was waiting for him in the foyer. When he walked through the door, she held out her arms and he walked to her and just allowed her to hug him. "Was it her?"

"I think so, but she won't answer me." His voice caught, and he squeezed his eyes shut. He wanted to be angry at her for doing this—wanted to be yell and scream—but instead, he felt defeated. His strings were pulled tight and waiting to break free. He stayed in the hug, but maneuvered Ali against the wall. Pressed up against her, pinning her, his lips claimed hers. He kissed her in a way that demanded she be alive against him. He needed to *feel* alive.

She matched his intensity and pulled him further into the push and pull of demanding and giving. She allowed him to lead her in the dance of wills, and she surrendered to him. As he picked her up, and she wrapped her legs around him, he knew without a doubt she was exactly what he needed. She was, in that very moment, the life that kept him going.

He laid her on the bed, never giving an inch of space between them. Ali's legs locked behind his back and her pulling him tightly to her was all the encouragement he needed.

He ached with passion between them. He needed release and was forcing himself to slow down.

"Don't hold back," she whispered as she moved her lips to his neck and nibbled. She unlocked her legs, and he moved just long enough to pull the clothes from each of them. She laid there watching him, letting him set the pace.

"Ali..." His eyes wandered over her body and his breathing deepened.

She reached for him, and as soon as her warm hand circled around his need, he nearly exploded. She guided him to her. She was ready for him, and he thrust deep inside her. Both of them moved into a primal mode and lost themselves in the movement with the other, passion matching passion until they were over the edge and spent.

He laid there still, half covering her for what seemed like forever. He was exhausted, but when he felt her shiver, he pushed himself off her. They had been so caught up in the movement, they hadn't bothered to pull back the covers on the bed.

As soon as she went to clean up, he got to his feet to pull back the covers. Things had happened so quickly that they hadn't had time. Once the bed was ready for sleeping, he laid down again. He needed her next to him tonight, *all* night, so when she came back in the room, he patted the spot beside him. She stood at the end of the bed, and he watched her, waiting for her reaction.

"Ready to get some sleep?" She walked slowly toward him. He nodded, and she grinned as she settled into the middle of the bed. "Good, because I need to be warmed up."

With a sigh of relief, Dawson curled up around her, spooning her petite form as they drifted off to sleep. For the second time in two nights, he slept soundly. There was no tossing and turning, and no nightmares with mutilated faces morphing into Sara's.

Wes's warmth covered Ali as he wrapped her in a cocoon made up of his body and the covers. Her need for him had grown, and although she'd tried to fight it, just like before, she couldn't say no. She didn't want to.

She allowed her mind to wander back to the feel of him: His muscles that flexed as he had lifted her, the tightness of his abs, and the solidness of his chest.

She exhaled slowly.

It was more than just his physical traits. She'd never met a man like Wes. Someone who was conscientious and caring, despite the gruff exterior. She knew his heart had broken over his sister. She felt it every time he had a new victim and was just waiting for the next one to be Sara.

Ali's heart ached for him. She wanted to protect him in some ways from any additional pain that finding his sister might bring, and Ali finally felt she was emotionally strong enough to help him.

After her last relationship took a turn for the worst and had ended horribly, she'd been guarded and hadn't wanted to let anyone in. Then Wes walked into her life and everything changed.

She sighed, completely content, and drifted off with heated thoughts of the man lying next to her.

The phone rang.

"Damn it!" Dawson swore. He glanced at the clock. At least it was six in the morning instead of five when the phone woke him, but he still wasn't in the mood to be awakened this way. Still, the blasted thing kept ringing.

Ali moaned softly as she turned to face him. "Are you going to answer that damn thing?"

"Man, you're a grump when you wake up in the morning." He reached for the phone. "Dawson."

"It's Brown. Another one. I'm texting you the address." The phone disconnected before Dawson could respond. He stared at what Brown had texted, and Dawson thought he was going to be sick.

Katie.

"What is it?" Ali was on the edge of the bed with her arm around him.

"Another one. Our time ran out."

"Shit." Ali was up and out of the bed, getting dress as she moved. "I'm going with you."

They were out the door and arrived at the small cottage where he'd left Katie last night. Brown was at the entrance waiting for them. "Captain's inside."

They passed into the house and saw Jenna sitting at the kitchen table. Her eyes were red from crying. They continued through the kitchen into the living room and found the body lying on the couch.

"Do you know who this is?" Collins spoke without looking up at them.

"I assume it's Katie O'Shannahan, sir," Dawson answered.

"Why would you assume that?" Collins turned to face him.

"Because I brought her here last night." Dawson met the man's eyes. "And then I left."

"You know this is not going to go over well."

"What I know is we have a woman dead the day after her husband beat her because he was angry about press showing up at their house, and she was too scared to tell the police it was him." Dawson took a deep breath. "What I know, sir, is Mr. O'Shannahan just landed himself back on the suspect list."

Dawson moved past the captain and stood next to the body. Ali was already there checking it over. "Same type of death. I assume we're looking at the same killer. Ten to eleven slashes to the face. I can tell you more once I get her back to the morgue."

Dawson felt defeated. "Thanks." He walked around the scene. There was no sign of a struggle. He made his way back to the kitchen and sat down next to Jenna. "Did you hear anything last night?"

She shook her head. "Katie and I had a couple of glasses of wine, caught up on the years we hadn't talked. She wouldn't tell me about the bruise on her face. She was very careful not to talk about her husband, and I didn't ask questions about him. He was the reason she and I lost contact."

Dawson nodded. "What time did you go to bed?"

"It was about ten. Between the wine and the long day I'd had at work, I was exhausted. Katie said she was going to sleep, too. I went to my room. She stayed on the couch." Jenna paused to collect herself. She trembled in shock. "I came out this morning and... found...her."

Dawson clenched his hands to his side, then relaxed

them. If this was Finn, he'd pay for this. First Katie's father, and now her.

Dawson left Jenna with a female officer as he went back to the living room. He checked the sliding door. Locked. He went into the laundry room off the living room. Door was locked there also. There didn't appear to be any sign of struggle or break in. How did he get inside?

He started for the door when Collins joined him on the steps. "Look, I know you don't want me going after O'Shannahan," Dawson said, "but I'm working with you, not for you. My goal is to catch a killer and if he's in my way right now as a suspect, I will bring him in and question him."

"I'm not saying don't go after him." Collins put his hand on Dawson's arm, stopping him. "I'm saying I'm more concerned that you were involved more in this victim's life and it could be a conflict of interest. I don't want your neck out there either."

"I was doing the right thing to try and keep her safe. I watched to make sure no one was following us. Do we know if she made any phone calls?" Dawson paused, frustrated beyond belief. "Was her GPS on in her cell phone? He could have tracked her any number of ways."

Collins nodded and started walking again. "I know you've got this, but be assured I've got your back on this. I agree with you that he is prime suspect number one. I'll go get him myself."

Dawson frowned. This was his case, and he was a bit irritated that the captain suddenly wanted to insert himself into the questioning only because the man was a politician. It wouldn't go well if Dawson found he was being blocked from doing his job just because of the captain not wanting to rock the boat. This fight had just become personal as far as Dawson was concerned, and no one should be in his way.

thirty-eight

Dawson strode into the police station and saw the captain leaning against a desk in the bullpen. He stood and pointed to room one. "He's in there. I haven't told him his wife is dead. I'll leave it to you."

Dawson gave a brief nod, watching the captain. "Anything else?"

"No. I'm not getting in your way. I thought he'd be a bit more peaceful if I brought him in, that's all. Go tear him apart if you want." Collins walked off without another word.

Turning toward the interrogation room, Dawson squared his shoulders and prepared for battle. He closed the door quietly behind him. Finn O'Shannahan was facing the door, sitting at the table with his hands folded.

"What am I doing here again?" Finn snarled with his voice raised louder than necessary.

Dawson moved to the chair across from him. He sat down and simply watched the man for a few minutes.

"Well?" Finn thundered.

Dawson sat back and crossed his ankles under the table. "Well, sir, I'm here to inform you that your wife, Katie, is dead."

The man didn't flinch. "What do you mean?"

"Dead. Passed on. Will no longer be coming back to your home."

"I want to see her." Finn started to stand.

"Sit down." Dawson spoke sharply—more so than he intended.

Finn dropped back into the chair. "Where was she?"

Dawson studied him. There didn't appear to be any surprise on his face, nor did he display any sadness or remorse. "She was found at a friend's home this morning."

"Who did it?"

"That's what I'd like to know. What do you want to share with me?"

"Are you kidding? You think I killed my wife?" Finn slammed both hands down on the table. "How dare you!"

"Oh, I dare. Your wife showed up here yesterday, looking like her face was hit with a battering ram from someone very angry, and now she's dead. Yes, I very much dare to wonder if you did it, and I will get the answers I need." Although angry, Dawson kept his voice steady and low, a much more dangerous combination than losing control.

"I want a lawyer," Finn stated.

"Fine." Dawson got up and left the room. He hollered to Brown, "Let him call his lawyer, but he's not to leave."

"Yes, sir. Where will you be?"

"Across the street at the ME's office. I need some answers before the lawyer gets here." Dawson held up his phone. "Text me if the lawyer arrives before I get back."

He jogged across the street and down the sterile hallway that he was getting to know so well, and yet still hated just as much. He poked his head into Ali's office, but she wasn't there. He then turned toward the autopsy room and found her. Her face was covered with a mask, and she moved around the corpse making comments into a recorder, assessing the body before starting the autopsy itself.

She stopped when she saw him. "I don't have much yet."

"A time of death?"

"Midnight, give or take an hour. Closest I can get at the moment."

He stared at the body. Katie had finally made a decision to get away from the abuse, and her life was cut short. How many times had he dreamed that he would be standing here identifying his sister?

"You did everything you could, Wes." Ali's voice broke through his thoughts.

"Did I? How did he find her?"

"You're assuming Finn did this. All we really know right now is that it's the same killer. And you couldn't tie him to the others."

Dawson acquiesced. "I know. Katie told me she'd prayed it was him. And I know that he left that bruise on her face, even if she didn't admit it. How does a man do that to his wife, or to any woman? I hope it is him. I want to nail his ass to the wall."

"I never understood that myself, but you know it's not uncommon. You've probably seen it more than I have." She moved closer. "You did what you could to make her safe, Wes. You can't be there every second for everyone that needs you."

"I'm not doing a good job at being there for anyone at all right now."

She scoffed. "Really? You're working yourself to the bone, working all day on the case and searching for hours almost every night for Sara. And then, you took the time to help Katie bury her father, and you tried to keep her safe by taking her to her friend's. Sounds to me like you're looking out for quite a few people."

He smiled. "You always know the right thing to say, don't you?"

"It's a gift." She winked. "Now get out so I can do my job."

He rolled his eyes and left. He returned to the precinct just as Finn's lawyer was introducing himself to the captain.

"I'd like my client released, unless you're charging him."

Captain glanced at Dawson, then put his attention back on the lawyer. "I haven't had a chance to ask him any questions. Are you saying you're going to have your client cooperate with the police regarding his wife's murder?"

"It's my understanding you'd already questioned him."

"He didn't answer any questions. He simply wanted to call you. We allowed that, of course, but I'm hoping you'll permit the questioning now that you're here. Time is of the essence for us to put together a timeline of when his wife was attacked."

Dawson followed the two men into the interrogation room and Finn stood up, glaring at his lawyer. "About time you got here."

His lawyer gestured to the chair. "Have a seat. The detective has a few questions for you."

Finn glared at his attorney. "Are you telling me I need to sit through this bullshit when they should be out looking for the person who did this to my poor Katie?"

Dawson held back a snort. "Mr. O'Shannahan, can you tell me where you were last night?"

"I was home, waiting for my wife to get back."

"And, where was she?" Dawson watched him carefully.

"I have no idea. I just found she was at someone else's house." Finn smirked.

"Was anyone with *you?*" Dawson asked.

"No." Finn looked at his lawyer. "Are we done? I really would like to see my wife."

The attorney glanced at Dawson. "Anything else at the moment?"

Dawson shook his head. "But please be available if more questions come up."

The lawyer stood. "Of course."

Finn rose from his chair and faced Dawson. "Do your job and get off my ass about this crap."

The lawyer touched his arm. "Finn, please no more."

Finn jerked away and stalked out of the room.

Dawson raised an eyebrow at the attorney. "You'll be hearing from us. You can let Mr. O'Shannahan know he'll be able to see his wife's body as soon as the autopsy is done."

Once the room was empty, Dawson slid into the chair. This wasn't going to be easy. Finn now had ties to three of the four victims. The question was, what was the tie to the diner owner?

thirty-nine

Dawson had spent the night at the police station, going through different scenarios. The only connection he couldn't make to Finn O'Shannahan was the diner and its owner, Charlie, their third victim. That seemed too coincidental, and Dawson was determined to find something to make that connection.

His phone rang. "Dawson."

"Hi, Detective Dawson. This is Cheryl at City Hall. I just wanted to let you know the plans you requested will take a little time to get. They're archived."

"Yes, you told me that when I made the request."

"Yes, but we're looking at a bit longer. They're having trouble finding the original plans. I'll let you know as soon as we can get them."

"I'd appreciate it if you could put a rush on this." Dawson hung up, shaking his head. He knew asking for a rush was pointless with city bureaucracy.

He looked at the board in front of him. It held colored pins for locations of deaths, and black pins for the addresses he was given. The diner was the one location without a connection to O'Shannahan and the address on the other side of the tracks—Beth's parent's house—had no connection either. There had to be one somewhere.

Dawson laid out the pictures of the victims on the table in front of him. All similar patterns to the face. He assumed the killer was right-handed, with the way the blade marks went. Although they crisscrossed over the face in total mutilation, the angle gave the impression of a right-handed swing. All blows were centered around the eyes. Rage. Considering the way the faces were destroyed, this killer was full of it. With the exception of Katie. The blows to her face seemed a bit softer. Maybe they'd been done without so much fury. Would Finn have been gentler with her because she was his wife?

As Dawson looked at the pictures, he concluded that the blows to Eugene were also shallower. Again, leading to the conclusion that there was a bit of a soft spot for these two victims, or at least, not the rage that the other victims felt.

"Anything new?" Captain Collins spoke from the door. His eyes had blackened smudges underneath them, likely from lack of sleep. Dawson knew this case was going to be front and center in the public eye once it was out that Finn was a prime suspect.

"There's rage with the middle two victims. But one and four seem softer in the intensity of the blows."

"Those two were related, right?"

"Yes, sir. Father and daughter." Dawson stared at the pictures.

"Do you have any doubt it was O'Shannahan?"

"Unfortunately, I *do* have doubts. I can't connect him to the third victim, or that location at all. The diner was one of the addresses that had been given to us. Although I can't connect him to the other address either."

"Recap for me then, how much is he connected to any of them?" Collins wasn't impatient, but demanding.

"Victim one and four were his father-in-law and wife.

Out of the addresses we received, one was his building. He was having an affair with victim two. Victim three, no connection to him or the other two addresses. So basically, four out of seven regarding connections. Not enough to arrest him for it."

"Damn. I want this wrapped up. What else do you have?"

"The other connection we have is victim three owned address two and was related to address three. But being connected to them doesn't do much since he's dead."

"And locations of deaths?" Collins asked.

"Alley across from the diner, alley down the street, outside the diner, and the residence. Private house is really out of the norm here from the others. Everything was outside, except that one. That one was high risk, given the fact that there were other people in the house. How did no one see or hear anything?"

"So basically, we're still stuck at square one with no concrete evidence that allows us to arrest anyone?" It was asked, but sounded more like a statement, so Dawson didn't answer and decided to move on to something else.

"I requested the plans for O'Shannahan's building we searched."

"Why?"

"Call it a gut feeling. A hunch. There was something in that building that's related to this. I *just* know it."

"We searched it thoroughly. There was nothing there." Collins paused, eyeing Dawson. "I know you want to solve this quickly…I want that also, however, don't be looking for evidence that isn't there. It's a waste of time."

Dawson nodded, but knew he wasn't going to listen to that. He'd learned through the years that in the hard cases, you had to listen to your gut. It typically panned out with something that had been overlooked. "I want this killer off the street, and if there's something that will connect O'Shannahan to all of the victims, I'm going after him."

"Don't let me stop you. Just stay on the track that has some actual facts with it. Hunches don't always pan out."

Dawson walked away before he said something he'd regret. Frustration filled him from the lack of respect from the captain over the lack of leads in this case. Every day that passed was making it more and more difficult to find something. With another victim, Dawson felt helpless. How did all this tie together?

There was no doubt regarding the ties between Finn and Katie, as well as Katie and Eugene, but beyond that there wasn't much. In some very obscure way, Katie and Darla could be tied together simply through Finn, but that still left out Charlie.

The stories of Lizzie Borden flashed through Dawson's mind. The MO was the same, but what was her motive for killing? She killed her father and stepmom. Were there others? If there were, were they just unknown?

Dawson was tired, *exhausted* really. The stress was hitting him hard. Luckily, he hadn't run into Sara in any of these deaths, but that just spurred him to get out and search for her more. Still, burning the candle at both ends was burning him out.

forty

Another day of chasing nothing. The autopsy of Katie didn't produce anything they didn't already know. Other than mutilation to the face, Katie was a normal, healthy, young woman with a few old bruises on her body.

"Did Finn beat her?" Dawson asked. The anger coursing through him was becoming way too familiar.

"This bruising is indicative of trauma. It could be from a hit, but they're old, and you know, there's no concrete evidence that Finn hit her." Ali glanced at him.

Dawson swore under his breath and paced back and forth in the autopsy room. "What do we know then?"

"Wes." Ali's soft voice broke through his thoughts. "Take a step back."

He looked around. "What?"

"From the case. Just for a second. Take a step back." After she pulled a sheet up over Katie, Ali gestured for him to follow her.

He trailed behind her into her office. "You know—"

She put a finger to his mouth. "Just stop. Right there. Sit down."

He dropped into the chair and waited.

"Take a deep breath," she whispered. She was standing in front of him, her eyes closed as she inhaled deeply.

He smiled. God, she was beautiful, and despite how frustrated and cranky he was, she was taking time out of her day to try and balance him. He reached out and grabbed her hands.

She smiled, but kept her eyes closed. He wanted to pull her to him, yet watched her instead as she inhaled deeply again and exhaled slowly.

She squeezed his hands. "Deep breaths," she said softly.

He closed his eyes and mimicked her breathing, slow and deep. Her positive, reassuring energy permeated him through the warmth of her hands and the heat of her body—so close, yet not touching him. He took a few more breaths and opened his eyes. Ali was standing there smiling and holding his hands—just watching him.

He grinned at her. "How do you do that?"

"Do what?"

"You have this calming effect on me. You just seem to know what I need, when I need it."

She shrugged. "I told you before, you're not the mystery you think you are."

He squeezed her hands before letting go. "Somehow, I should take that as an insult, yet you make it sound like a compliment."

"Take it whatever way you feel better about it." She moved to her chair and sat down. "I know you're frustrated, Wes. And I get it, I really do. But you need to stop spinning your wheels. Go outside the box and look beyond the connection between the victims and Finn."

"Now you're just sounding like the captain." Dawson shook his head. "I don't know how else to go about this."

"Okay. Well, there's no connection between Finn and all the victims, right?"

"Right." He raised an eyebrow at her.

"Look at something else then. What else could be a common thread among them? Or Who?"

He sighed. "You think I haven't tried that?"

"I think you *think* you have. But I also know you get tunnel vision."

"What?" He chuckled. "I don't get tunneled vision."

She looked at him. "No? You're pretty homed in on Finn. You're so convinced that he has something to do with it, that you aren't looking beyond."

"Come on, Ali. That's not fair." He snaked his fingers through his hair.

"Fair or not, you know there's some truth to it. I'm just saying I think there's something we're missing."

"We, huh?" He stood, then leaned toward Ali and put his hands on the arms of her chair. "I like the sound of that." He bent forward and kissed her gently before turning and heading out the door.

He didn't need to look back at her to know she was smiling. They were on the same page, and although he was still fighting his feelings, it was comforting to know he had someone in his corner—and someone who had his back.

I'd barely gotten into the room before the migraine hit me hard. Hard enough it took me to my knees. The pain was unbearable, and as I laid there on the floor, the flashes of memories started again. The woman—the one who kept showing up—kept yelling at me. I was always doing something wrong. Why? Why was she yelling at me?

I told her over and over again that I didn't do it, but of course she didn't believe me. Of course, not. She never did. She always acted like she was better than me, but she wasn't. We were the same, both of us. Father destroyed our lives, and there was no getting around that. I saved both of us, and she refused to give me any credit. Instead, all I continued to get was yelling, threatening to never talk to me again.

The pain mingled with lights flashing. I closed my eyes, trying to stop it and squeezed my hands to my head, like that would keep the pain from coming. Finally, the black ascended and took the pain away as I drifted into oblivion.

I don't know how long I slept. I opened my eyes slowly. The room was dark, except for the glow from my cell phone. I reached for it and saw the time. 6:00 p.m. It would be dark outside soon and I could hopefully accomplish what I needed to do. I just wanted out of this damn city. Away from everyone who knew me and looked down on me.

The migraine and memories had left me weak. The pain was gone, but the exhaustion lingered. These episodes were coming more often now. I didn't know how to stop them and had no idea what these memories meant. I didn't remember anything that ever flashed in my mind. It was like watching someone else's life.

I slowly sat up and pulled my knees to my chin. Wrapping my arms around my legs, I sat there and tried to focus on the memories. I never could seem to recall the details after the migraine was gone. I'd been trying so hard lately to place the pictures, the people in these flashes. A woman—not that old—maybe in her thirties. A man who I had the impression was my father, yet looked nothing at all like him. He had the same look in his eyes, though, as my father did when he'd come to my room.

I rocked back and forth. I hated remembering what he'd done to me. I despised him.

I hated the life I had, the one I'd had no choice but

to live all these years. A life handed to me as a child that I couldn't escape. I needed to escape. That need was becoming more and more insistent within me.

With the anger starting to boil again, I stood. Near the wall, lay my list. I picked it up and looked at it. Two names left. One of those would be gone tonight. I was done waiting. My hatchet leaned against the wall next to my cloak and gloves. I smiled. They'd become my lifeline without even knowing it. They gave me hope, hope for the future and a new life.

I laid down on the floor and rested. I had a few hours to kill. I didn't want this left-over migraine effect to interfere with my big night. Time passed as I laid there on the hard floor. Although not being able to drift back off to sleep, I felt rested, and my mind was once again clear. I quickly glanced at my phone which showed that it was now 10:00 p.m. Time to prepare myself for the next kill.

I pulled on the dark cloak that allowed me to blend with the blackness of night. The gloves were soft and pliable in my hands, as I slowly caressed them before sliding them on. Their softness grounded me. I closed my eyes and allowed the heaviness of the cloak on my shoulders and the malleability of the gloves to boost my confidence—the uncertainty of my life slipping away. Lastly, I opened my eyes and reached for the hatchet.

It had weight to it, but wasn't too heavy. I tightened my grip around the handle and lifted it above my head. It was a victory gesture. I wasn't an evil person. I knew that deep down I was a product of my bad childhood. I just wanted to be heard, to hold people accountable for the acts they'd committed. Why was that so wrong?

It was time. I pulled the hood up over my head and exited the building. The streets were dark. The budget cuts and the way the city was just rundown had been a blessing for me. No streets lamps had been repaired. Alleys were overrun with homeless people. Anyone who had any common sense had vacated the city long ago, and now it was an empty shell of its former bright self.

I arrived at my car, blending in with the shadows and still not meeting anyone. This car was a piece of junk, but it wouldn't be long and I'd be able to leave this behind, just like my life here and all the unhappy memories from the past.

I drove the side streets until I arrived at my destination. Parked on a logging road at the edge of the woods, I made my way with my hatchet in hand hidden among the folds of my cloak, until I arrived at the side door. The building was dark. Most residents would likely be asleep by now.

I entered the room quietly and stood at the doorway, allowing my eyes to adjust. The main door to the hallway was closed, and I crept across the room to lock it. Turning toward the woman in the bed, I saw her watching me.

"You were expecting me." It was a statement, but I watched her closely for any reaction.

She nodded, barely perceptible, but it triggered a smile to come to my face. "Are you scared?" I didn't usually interact with my victims, but I was curious about this one. She tried to smile and shake her head no. Again, barely a movement, but I recognized it. I wish she'd just speak and tell me why she wasn't scared. That fact—her lack of fear—irked me. I wanted her scared, fearful for her life. And yet, she laid there, waiting.

I pulled the hatchet from the folds of my cloak. Her eyes wandered to it, then back to me. There was still no fear. Just an understanding, and what? What else was that look? Pity? I didn't want her pity.

I heard the first toll of the clock, marking the eleven o'clock hour. I raised the hatchet, ready for my first swing, and I hesitated. In that second, she grasped my free hand, and I looked down to where she held it. She squeezed and gave a little nod. My instinct was to pull away, but she had nothing left to live for, and I was ready to give her want she wanted…deserved.

I allowed her to hold my hand as I brought the hatchet down with the other. The first swing hit the mark of her forehead, across her left eye. She flinched, but continued to hold my hand. Still, there was no fear.

I closed my eyes for a brief moment and swung ten more times. Eleven. I finished just as the bell stopped marking the passage of time. By the eleventh stroke, her hand had fallen away from mine. I knew the exact moment death had claimed her.

I stood there, staring down at her. The blood—warm and pooling on her pillow—didn't have the same effect on me as it had with the others. This one was different. Her only crime had been indifference to me. In a brief passing second, a twinge of guilt struck me.

"It didn't have to be this way," I whispered and ran for the outside door. I stopped when I heard the jiggling of the handle of the other door. Thankfully, I'd locked it. The nurse outside the door yelled for help.

I turned and fled the scene.

I knew this particular kill would be the one that wouldn't be lying there for hours waiting for someone to find them. Getting back to my car, and once behind the wheel, I sat there for a moment. My eyes closed, recalling the feel of her hand in mine. Anger surged. She deserved every blow she received and so much more. She wasn't better than the rest of them. I'd seen over the years how they treated people more unfortunate than themselves, the judgment they bestowed on everyone around them.

No, I was glad she was gone. She was just another one who'd no longer judge me.

"Did you do it?" The voice was in my head again. I could see that woman asking me…was it me? Who was she talking to? The migraine started again, and I knew I needed to get back home before it was full-blown. These flashes and migraines were happening with less and less time between them. Was I going crazy?

I put the car in drive and sped down the logging road and headed for home. I'd cross the name off my list tomorrow.

forty-one

Dawson had no sooner stepped through the door to his house when a text came through that there was *another one*. He ran his fingers through his hair as a sigh of frustration escaped him.

Not another one. This murder happened at the Sunnyside Nursing Home.

He paused, staring at the messaged address. He glanced at his watch to note the time; fifteen past midnight.

As he drove into the parking lot at the nursing home, he realized this was the place Mrs. Murray lived. As he exited his car, he called to Brown who was coming out of the building.

"What've we got?"

"Elderly lady, same MO as all the others. But it doesn't seem as violent somehow."

Dawson nodded and waited for Brown to continue.

Brown smiled. "You might be surprised to learn her name."

"Well, don't keep me in suspense, Brown."

"Mary Murray."

Dawson gaped at him. "Mary Murray. The lady who couldn't speak because of a stroke?"

"Yep."

Dawson looked at Brown, puzzled. "Why was she the target?"

"I don't know, sir."

Dawson shot Brown a withering look at the sir. "Remind me of her room number?"

Brown looked at his notebook. "111."

"Thanks." This was a link to Charlie, the diner's owner, but he might be hard-pressed to find the connection to any of the other victims, and probably not to Finn O'Shannahan. He just prayed this wasn't another dead end.

He walked into Room 111. To his right, a nurse sobbed quietly into a towel. A suited man stood next to her just watching. Ali was at the bed, bent over Mrs. Murray.

"Same killer?" Dawson murmured quietly as he stood next to Ali.

"I would say so. Definitely eleven blows to the face. See these blows though, they aren't as violent as the other victims. More like Katie's. These two are different. Same MO, but either the killer knew Katie and this one, or we could be looking at two different killers."

"Jesus, Ali, don't say there could be another one. We can't even find one killer, let alone two." He gestured with his head towards the nurse and man. "Who's the suit?"

"Owner of the nursing home. He's waiting to talk to you."

Dawson turned and made his way over to the man and woman. "I take it you found Mrs. Murray, miss?"

The nurse wiped at her tears and took a deep breath. "Yes, the door was locked, which I thought was odd when I was making my rounds. By the time we got it open, no one was here, but the side door was open."

"What time was this?"

"About 11:20 or 11:30. It took us about fifteen minutes to get in because the lock was jammed and the key wouldn't work."

"And no one went outside the building to come in the side door?" Dawson pointed at the door.

"It's usually locked. I don't know how someone could have gotten in that way."

Dawson tried hard to not roll his eyes. He turned to the man who appeared to be bored with the whole thing. "And you are?"

"Victor Donahue. Owner." The man stuck out his hand and Dawson looked at it and back to the man's face before shaking it.

"And just when did you get here?"

"A few minutes before you. I came as soon as I was called."

"Okay. I'm sure I'll have questions for you later, but now, why don't you go wait in the office and I'll come find you."

"I need to sit around and wait? It's late. Maybe we could just talk tomorrow."

Dawson looked at him. "I'm sure your resident's family would appreciate you cooperating with us, unless you'd rather wait for a lawsuit from them about the outside door being unlocked."

The man scowled. "I'll be in the office."

Dawson turned and walked away from him. Brown was standing in the doorway and Dawson pointed to the nurse and Mr. Donahue. "Stay with them in the office, please, Brown."

"Yes, sir."

Dawson rolled his eyes and turned toward Ali. "What else do you have?"

"Given the time they found her, I'd say it had just happened...time close to 11:00 p.m."

231

He moved around to the other side of the bed and studied the body. "What do you make of that?" He pointed at the right hand.

The fingers were curled like she'd been holding onto something. "The others weren't like that. She either had something in her hand that the perp took, or she was holding onto the perp while she was being killed."

"There aren't any defensive wounds?" Dawson questioned.

"None. In fact, the blows to the face are softer than the others, like I said before. My gut says this had a different kind of feeling to it. Not rage. No violence. But that doesn't help us."

"I need to go talk to her husband and daughter."

"Do you know them?"

"You know Beth, the waitress with the sparkling personality?"

Ali nodded.

"Our vic's daughter."

"Dawson…" He glanced at her. Her hair was pulled back as she always wore it while working, but her face was soft as she looked at him. "Be nice."

He grinned. "I'm always nice." He grew serious, and he raised his hand at her. "I know. It's her mother."

"I'll keep you posted when I can get her to the morgue and can look closer at the blade marks." Ali's remarks were made as she turned back to the body. She'd already dismissed him, which was one of the reasons he was falling for her. She was just as much in the zone as he was when he was working.

He headed to the office where the owner and nurse were waiting. He entered and gestured for Brown to come to the door. "All quiet?"

"Yes, sir."

Dawson rubbed the back of his neck. "I'll finish up with these two. Go ahead and look outside the side door to see if there's any indication of forced entry." He waited until Brown had left the office, then turned toward the two sitting at the desk.

Dawson smiled. "Miss, are you able to talk more now about what you found?"

"Yes," she said. "I'm Julie." Visibly shaken, she was sitting on the edge of one of the two chairs facing the desk.

He sat down beside her in the other chair. The owner sat behind the desk, leaning back. He looked like this was the last place he wanted to be.

"Tell me what you'd been doing before starting your rounds," Dawson said to Julie.

She sighed. "Just the usual. I go through the charts to make sure everything is signed off on from the day shift, medications dispensed. Things like that. After that, I typically check on each patient. Most of them are sleeping by then, but I peek in their rooms and shut off main lights and make sure night lights are on. I usually close their doors for the night after I've checked on them."

"Are doors always open during the day?" Dawson asked.

Julie's eyes widened. "No, some patients prefer their doors to stay shut during the day. There are many patients that don't get a lot of visitors and they don't like to see people walking in the halls."

"And Mrs. Murray? Did she usually have her door open?"

"Sometimes. She was nonverbal. She never seemed to express a preference and was really one who just laid there. Never wanted for anything. Her husband stopped coming when he was no longer able to get here on his own. Her daughter came occasionally, but lately it was less and less."

"When was the last time either of them were here?"

Julie thought for a moment. "I honestly don't know. It's been a while."

"When was the last time she had a visitor?"

"Actually, it was you, sir. No one has been to see her since the day you came to talk to her."

He sat back in the chair. This poor woman had been alone with no visitors, and now she'd died a violent death. His heart ached, thinking of Sara being alone. Yes, she wasn't in a nursing home, but she could be somewhere by herself thinking no one cared for her.

He turned toward Victor Donahue. The man gave the impression of being a snake. He'd just had a death in his establishment, and he had the gall to looked bored with the whole thing.

"How often are you here, Mr. Donahue?" Dawson asked.

"Not often. I have a manager to deal with the day-to-day. The only reason they called me tonight is because of the severity of the death."

"Severity of the death?" Dawson stared at him. "So, you aren't usually notified when a resident passes away?"

"It's in a weekly report I receive, but this is a nursing home with elderly people. Deaths are part of the daily routine."

"So how often are you in the building, Mr. Donahue?"

"Couple of times a year, I guess." He shrugged. "Like I said, I have a manager who handles the day-to-day operation."

"Have you had problems before with people breaking in through outside doors and into patient rooms?"

"Of course not. That has never happened."

The door to the office opened and Brown stepped in. "Sir, the door in Mrs. Murray's room didn't lock. It had been tampered with so it wouldn't."

Dawson turned back to the owner. "Were you aware of this?"

"No, I wasn't. That is unacceptable."

Dawson stared at him a second. "And who is responsible for maintenance of those doors?"

"Well, the manager would have that information."

Dawson stood. "Basically, sir, you don't have a clue about this establishment other than taking the money from these people who probably can't afford to be here." It wasn't a question, but a statement. "You're free to go. Leave your contact information with Officer Brown so I can reach you if I have more questions."

Dawson glanced at his watch before heading to the parking lot. 3:30 a.m. It was early still, but he needed to notify the husband and Beth, if she was around. She'd told Dawson she didn't live with her father so he had no address for her.

Dawson paused as the body was brought out to be transported to the morgue.

Ali stopped next to him. "Just leaving now?"

"Got questioning the owner and nurse. I'm about to head to Mr. Murray's house. Want to tag along?"

"Can you drop me off at the morgue after?"

"Of course."

She nodded. "Let me just tell Dan to go ahead and I'll meet him there later."

Dawson and Ali started for the other side of town, headed to the Murray's house. It was now close to 4:00 a.m. He hated to wake them, but they needed to know. The lights were off in their home as he expected when he pulled up in front.

They got out slowly and approached the door. Dawson rang the doorbell, but not hearing it, he knocked as loud as he could without pounding. He waited five minutes, then succumbed and pounded on the door. Still no answer.

"Do you have a phone number for him or Beth?" Ali asked.

"No." He beat on the door again. He heard a shuffling sound inside before a light came on.

The door cracked open and Dawson could barely see Mr. Murray on the other side. "Yeah?"

"Mr. Murray, I'm Detective Wes Dawson, I was here the other day. And this is Ali Jenson. Sir, can we come in and talk to you, please?"

"She's not here."

"Who, sir?"

"Beth. She don't live here."

Dawson glanced at Ali. "Sir, we're not looking for Beth. I'm here to talk to you."

The door swung open slowly and Dawson stepped to the side to let Ali precede him. He closed the door behind him as she moved nearer to Mr. Murray who sat down on the couch.

"Damn early for a visit, isn't it?" The man's voice shook, showing his age.

"Yes, sir, it is," Dawson said. "However, this is important. We have some bad news to share with you. Sir, your wife, Mary, was attacked at the nursing home this evening and has died."

"My Mary? She's not here?" Mr. Murray looked around, confused.

"No, sir," Ali said as she sat down next to him. "She was at the Sunnyside Nursing Home."

"I don't understand," he replied, looking at her.

She glanced at Dawson. "Mr. Murray, your wife has been at the nursing home for a while now. Do you remember that she had a stroke?"

A moment of clarity crossed his face. "I couldn't take care of her."

"No, sir. That's why she was at the nursing home."

Mr. Murray nodded. "Yes. Is she okay?" The confusion was gone, but Dawson was unsure how long that would last.

"Sir, she was the victim of an attack last night at the nursing home."

"An attack? Is she okay?" Mr. Murray looked at Dawson, then back to Ali.

Dawson drew a deep breath. "I'm sorry to say, sir, that she did not survive."

Understanding finally filled Mr. Murray's eyes as they pooled with tears. "Can I see her?"

Ali reached for Mr. Murray's hand. "Not right now. I think it would be best if you didn't see her at the moment." She looked at Dawson for back up.

He sighed. The brutal nature wasn't for anyone's eyes, and this type of unrecognizable damage was not for loved ones to see. Dawson had seen a lot in his career, and the mutilation of these faces made *him* a bit uneasy. Raw anger. "Sir, is there a way to reach your daughter so she can come be with you?"

The man's clarity was gone in an instant. "Beth. I think her and Mary went shopping."

Ali squeezed Mr. Murray's hand. "Sir, she's not with Mary. I think we need to call Beth to come be with you."

"I don't know her number." Mr. Murray looked at Ali. "Do I know you?"

"I'm Ali Jenson. I'm here with Detective Dawson about your wife." He nodded, but didn't seem to understand.

"Mr. Murray," Dawson began, "where does Beth live?"

"I don't remember." Mr. Murray started to stand. "Is something the matter with her? I knew she would always be in trouble."

"No, sir. There's nothing the matter. She's not in trouble," Dawson reassured him. Dawson was reaching for his phone to call Brown when the back door closed.

"Beth?" Mr. Murray called out.

"Yup. I just stopped by to do some laundry!" Beth hollered from the kitchen.

"Beth, could you come in here please?" Dawson called out.

She came through the kitchen door and stared at Dawson. "What are you doing here?" By the look on her face, she'd lost her animosity toward him.

"We stopped by to talk to your dad and you, about your mom." Dawson gestured toward Ali who was still sitting next to Mr. Murray.

"What about her?"

Dawson moved back a step and motioned for Beth to come and sit down. "I'm not sure your dad is understanding what we're telling him..."

"Just spill it. He's as senile as they get. He needs to be in the damn nursing home with her." Beth sat down in the chair, blatantly staying away from her father.

"Your mom was attacked last night, and unfortunately she didn't survive it." Dawson watched her closely.

Beth stared at him, then looked at her father. She stood and moved to sit next to him. "Dad, do you understand that Mom is gone?"

"Yes, she has to stay at the nursing home because of the stroke." He allowed Beth to hold his hand, and Ali quietly stood and moved away.

"No, Dad. This officer is saying she died last night." Beth spoke gently, as if speaking to a child. She held his hand as the man's eyes filled with tears again when clarity came.

"Do we need to identify her, or I guess the nursing home already did that?" Beth asked.

"No, it's been taken care of. We may have some questions for you later, but that can wait. We'll get out of here for now. Let us know if you need anything." Dawson placed his business card on the arm of the chair. "I'm sorry for your loss, Beth."

"Thank you." She turned back to her father, clearly dismissing them. But Dawson was surprised by her gentle tone with him, considering how their other encounters had gone. Maybe the family bonds ran deeper in most families than he realized. It was a refreshing look for Beth.

Dawson indicated toward the door with his head, and he and Ali quietly stepped outside.

forty-two

Dawson drove Ali to her office in silence. He could only imagine what she was thinking, but in his own mind he couldn't help but wonder how his parents would react if they were told that Sara was dead, or even how he'd react if he heard one of his parents had died. There had been no love lost between them, and he kept in touch out of obligation, not because of a deep family bond.

"You okay?" Ali's voice broke his thoughts as he pulled in front of the medical examiner's office.

He sighed. "Yeah. Thanks for going with me."

"Of course. We saw a very different side of Beth today." Ali reached for the door handle.

"A pleasant surprise." He smiled at her. "Let me know when you have any more information on Mrs. Murray."

Ali half smiled and was out of the car before either of them could say another word. He watched her walk into the building. She was a calming presence in his life, one that he'd been longing for as long as he could remember.

He glanced at the clock on the dashboard. Eight-thirty. He needed coffee and the stuff at the station wasn't going to cut it. He parked his car at the precinct and started strolling down the street. A new coffee shop had opened about a month ago and he had yet to try it. Maybe it would be the kick of decent caffeine that he needed.

He glanced around the shop as he entered. Not a lot of tables, but enough to make it cozy. He perused the menu and decided on an Americano, needing the extra jolt of caffeine. As he waited for it, his phone beeped indicating a text message. He glanced at it.

Plans are ready at the City Planner's office. A text from Brown.

He texted back a brief *ok*.

With coffee in hand, he headed for City Hall just down the street. In his gut, he felt that this was the missing key, but unsure as to how. Depending on what the plans showed, he might need access to the building again, and he wasn't sure Finn would be willing to let them go through it a second time. He headed back to the precinct, knowing he'd need Collins' help on bringing Finn in to open the building.

Arriving at the station, Dawson made his way to the conference room where he was set up. He laid out the blueprints on the table and studied it. He could pinpoint the rooms they'd searched. At the back of the building, off the small room that he remembered had a cot in it, was a smaller room. It could have been a closet, but Dawson had looked in it and knew it wasn't as big as the plans showed.

"Brown said you got the blueprints for O'Shannahan's building." Collins' voice brought Dawson around to face the door.

"I do. Can we get back into it?" Dawson gestured to the table. "Looks like there was another room we didn't go into."

"Why are you hung up on this building?" Collins walked to the table and looked at the blueprints.

"It's a gut feeling." Dawson raised his hand. "I know you said not to let my gut feelings influence me, but I can't shake this, and I think we need to follow it."

Collins pointed to the room that Dawson had been looking at. "This one?"

Dawson nodded. "When we were in this adjoining room, I had a feeling that something was there, but I didn't know about this room at the time. Look, I went and got these blueprints on a hunch, and I was right that there was more to this building than we saw."

Collins nodded slowly and watched Dawson. "You're sure about this?"

"Yes, sir." Dawson waited. "Can we go and look at it at least?"

"We'll have to get a search warrant. I don't think O'Shannahan will let us back in."

Dawson sighed. "Not even to help find his wife's killer?"

"I'll call him, but don't get your hopes up. If he says no, you're going to let this go. We'll never get a search warrant based on a gut feeling." Collins turned and left the room, leaving Dawson feeling even further away from catching this maniac.

Time had stopped it seemed, and Dawson was no closer to getting answers than he was before. This last murder seemed impossible to be a targeted victim. Who could possibly want to harm an elderly lady who couldn't speak or move?

He stared at the victimology board. Eugene, Darla, Charlie, Katie, and now Mary. What was the common thread? Charlie had been Mary's brother, and Darla hung out at the diner. And then Eugene and Katie were father and daughter, but how did they fit in with the other three? There had to be a common thread between them, and Dawson was wound tighter than a bow string, trying to figure it out.

"Dawson, get going." Collins voice from the door startled Dawson. "Finn will meet you at the house. He's not happy, but he wants his wife's killer caught. Take Brown with you. If you find something, let me know and I'll send a team out."

"Yes, sir."

"This better pay off, Dawson. My neck is on the line and I'm trusting your feeling. Quite honestly, we've got nothing else to go on."

Dawson and Brown arrived at the abandoned building just as Finn arrived. "Mr. O'Shannahan, thank you for allowing us access again."

Finn nodded but didn't say a word. He unlocked the door and followed Dawson and Brown into the building. Dawson went straight to the back room where the plans had showed the secret room. Once Finn had unlocked the door, Dawson went directly to the closet. He stepped inside. He pressed at both top corners and moved his hands methodically and slowly over every inch of the wood.

"Well?" Finn impatiently demanded.

Dawson ignored him as Brown tried to placate him. Dawson was halfway down the back of the wall on the right-hand side when his hand came to a rough patch, unlike the rest of the wood in the panel. "Brown, bring your flashlight over here."

As Brown shined the light into the closet, Dawson ran his hand over the area and pushed gently. There was a slight give, and Dawson pushed harder. A small area of the back panel swung open. It was just wide enough for him to squeeze through sideways. Brown followed him in and shined the light around the room. Dawson just stood there for a moment, taking in every corner of the small space.

"Call Collins and tell him to get a team down here," Dawson instructed Brown.

"What's in there?" Finn called.

"Sir, please stay there." Dawson moved into the middle of the room. It wasn't at all big—maybe twelve-by-twelve. There were no furnishings, but over by the back wall, a black crayon and a piece of paper caught his eye. He pulled a pair of latex gloves from his pocket and put them on, then picked up the paper. As he read it, his heart almost stopped. He'd found the key he needed.

His stomach turned. This wasn't complete though. More was coming, and he had to stop this killer in his tracks. "Brown, stay here and wait for Collins. Then meet me at 11 Highland Road. And get Finn out of this building."

Dawson moved back through the closet into the small room. Brown followed him. "Bag up that ratty blanket on that cot."

"Sir, what is it?" Brown asked.

"I'll explain later. Just hurry up and be ready to meet as soon as Collins gets here."

"What's going on?" Finn demanded.

"Sir, no time to explain. Please step outside and wait for Captain Collins." Dawson gestured to the door.

"I'm not going anywhere until you tell me what's going on?" Finn was belligerent. "Collins said you had a hunch, and I went with it. But damn it, if this leads to Katie's killer, I want to know."

Dawson sighed. "Mr. O'Shannahan, I want to get that killer as much as you do, but right now, I need to stop the next murder. I'll get you answers, but please, for the love of God, will you get outside now, and just for once, do what I ask you to?"

Finn stepped back as if Dawson had slapped him, but nodded slowly and walked ahead of him out of the building. Collins and a forensic team were just pulling up. Dawson gave the captain a quick rundown and told him to send Brown as soon as he could. Dawson threw up a prayer that he'd be in time as he sped across town.

forty-three

Dawson pulled up in front of 11 Highland Road. The house had no signs of activity, but it never did. He moved slowly up the front walk to the porch. Peering in the windows, he saw nothing. He contemplated his next move. If he knocked, he could tip off the killer if he was inside.

Brown pulled up, so Dawson went down to the road. "Stay at the front door. I'll head to the back," Dawson instructed Brown.

Dawson moved methodically around the house, peeking in windows as he came to them. No signs of life anywhere. A knot formed in his stomach, and he prayed he wasn't too late to stop this one. If Beth was here with her father, she was in danger, too. He didn't think he could handle it if he lost a whole family in the span of two days.

As he came to the back corner of the house, he peered around and took in the back yard. A driveway came up from the alley behind the house, and there was no car there. As he came around the corner, he saw that the back door was open a crack. He slowly pushed it fully open and stepped into the house. It was dark. Windows were covered with such filth; no sun could get through for any natural light. There were no lights on, and Dawson stood still until his eyes adjusted to the dimness.

He looked around at the kitchen where he stood. It was outdated and dirty. Dust covered the counters and cobwebs hung from the corners.

"Why are you doing this?" Mr. Murray's voice caught Dawson's attention.

He crept slowly to the door leading to the living room. Mr. Murray was facing the kitchen. Before him—with his back to Dawson—was a person in a dark cloak. The hood was up to shield the face. Dawson waited to hear the response.

"You know why." The voice was soft and feminine, and Dawson could barely make out the words.

The old man laughed. "You never could just enjoy it. Always just lying there crying, begging me to stop." The man's voice had a hint of strength to it that Dawson hadn't heard before. The feeble man was gone, and he was goading the killer. The man had raped this person, but Dawson still couldn't place the voice.

Dawson took another step forward as the killer brought an ax out from under the cloak. He raised a finger to his lips to shush the old man from saying anything, but the man ignored him and grinned at the killer. "You don't have the guts to kill me."

Dawson shook his head at Mr. Murray. Stop goading her. She raised the ax over her head and grasped it with her other hand as well to hold the handle.

The man smirked at the hatchet and stood taller. "How powerful you must have felt over my wife, as helpless as she was."

She waivered. "She deserved it."

Dawson stepped into the living room. "Drop the ax!"

The figure turned around and smiled at him. "Welcome, Detective Dawson. Finally. What fun I have had knowing you couldn't see what was right under your nose."

Beth. "Put down the ax, Beth."

"Call me Lizzie." She continued to keep the weapon raised above her head.

Lizzie. Lizzie Borden. He had *been chasing a ghost.* "Okay, Lizzie. Put the ax down."

She laughed. "You think that's going to make me want to stop without finishing my list?"

"I found your list. Tell me about it. Why Eugene?"

Puzzlement flashed in her eyes. "You mean that old man? The first one?"

Dawson nodded. "He wasn't on your list."

"No, he wasn't." She grinned. "He was my guinea pig."

Dawson grew sick. Brown opened the front door and came in, gun trained on Beth. "Okay. Why Darla?"

"She was a bitch. Bad mouthed me to every customer in that diner." She paused a moment, biting her bottom lip. "I wish she hadn't died so quickly. I would have liked it to be more painful for her."

"Couldn't let some negative comments go?" Dawson asked.

"No. Same with Charlie. I heard what he said to you that first day you talked to him. He was a bastard to work for. Just because he was family, he thought that gave him the right to treat me like the dirt beneath his boots."

"He wasn't very nice to you, no."

Beth frowned. "Neither were you. You baited me every chance you could. Maybe I should have put you on my list."

"I'm sorry about that, Beth. I was very wrong." Dawson frowned. "What about Katie?"

"That pretty lady you were so taken with?" Beth laughed. "She was just to throw a curveball at you. That was really fun because I had no resentment against her."

Dawson snarled. "Fun? You thought murdering an innocent person that had done nothing to you was *fun?*"

"Oh, Detective Dawson, don't let emotion cloud your thought process." Sweetness rolled off her voice before she started laughing.

He took a step closer, and Beth moved nearer to her father. "Don't come any closer. You may get a shot off, but I'll get one swing into him."

Dawson stopped. "And what about your mother?"

Beth nodded. "Yes, that one was a bit different for me. She knew why I was there and wasn't afraid. She actually nodded to me like she was saying, go ahead." Beth took a deep breath. "I even let her hold my hand while I killed her. She could've been safe. All she needed to do was protect me from him." She pointed at her father.

"Why? What did you need protecting from?" Dawson knew the answer already, but he had to keep her talking to figure out how to get that ax from her before she let a swing go. Her father was too close to her. She was right. There was a chance she could hit him once and could do some major damage, possibly even be fatal. He couldn't have another death at her hands.

"He...my own father...came into my room every night. Touched me, hurt me. I cried out so many nights for her to come rescue me, but no, she knew what was going on and took a sleeping pill every night so she wouldn't have to face it." Her voice rose an octave as her anger surged.

William Murray started laughing. "You were so pathetic thinking your mother would help you. She knew better than to interfere."

Beth turned and faced him, the hatchet twitching as her hands shook with rage. She took another step toward him.

"Beth, stop right there."

"It's Lizzie." Beth never looked at Dawson.

He trained his gun on her arm. "Lizzie. Stop. Don't make me shoot you."

She laughed, differently this time. It was a strange cackle that he couldn't quite place. The eeriness that came from it made him feel like he was caught in a time warp. She raised the ax a little higher and the shot rang out. Dawson had squeezed the trigger and the bullet tore through her shoulder. It went straight through and stopped as it penetrated the wall behind her.

The hatchet fell with a crash as Beth screamed and dropped to the floor. She held her shoulder, crying out in anguish.

Brown rushed forward to take Mr. Murray from the room, and Dawson walked over to where Beth laid on the floor.

"You should have let me finish the list," she panted out. "I was almost done and then I would have just gone away."

He kneeled beside her, then pulled his t-shirt off over his head and wrapped it around her shoulder, applying pressure. "Beth, why didn't you just leave town? Why take revenge like this?"

She closed her eyes. "Anger was the only thing that kept me alive. You wouldn't understand."

"*You have the right to remain silent. Anything you say can and will be used against you in a court of law. You have the right to an attorney…*" Dawson recited her rights as she laid there waiting for the ambulance.

He watched her in silence. He'd caught the ghost, but his guilt for all the lives he couldn't save hit him in waves. And the innocent ones: Eugene, a lonely man who just wanted to be near his daughter, Katie, who was caught up unknowingly in the evil.

As the ambulance drove off, Dawson closed his eyes. Exhaustion rolled over him as the letdown of the case finally being over hit him. He wanted nothing more than to get to Ali and just hold her.

acknowledgements

One of the many things I have learned from my children is that life is the greatest when you are out of your comfort zone. This is a story that has been in the works for quite some time and it definitely took me out of my comfort zone. This book would not have been written if not for the support of Jeanne Hardt and Jennifer Gatlin. These two ladies gave me the support and encouragement I needed to break into a new genre. The hours we spent brainstorming and talking through this book were priceless in helping me shape this book into the book I had envisioned. A very special thank you to Officer Carl Shrake for answering my endless questions and for the support in writing this story. As always, thanks to my three children for always believing in me.

about the author

E.L. REED moved to Tennessee after living in New Hampshire all her life. She has fond memories of the Maine coastline and incorporates the ocean into all her books. She has three grown children and is enjoying her empty nest. Her life has been touched and changed by her son's autism - she views life through a very different lens than before he was born. Growing up as an avid reader, it was only natural for Emma Leigh to turn to creating the stories for others to enjoy. Emma Leigh continues to learn through her children's strength and abilities that pushes her to go outside her comfort zone on a regular basis. She has also authored romantic suspense, women's fiction and co-authored children's books. She shares her love for writing as an English Professor at a local community college.

For more information, please visit elreedauthor.com

ALSO AVAILABLE FROM
EMMA LEIGH REED

AVAILABLE WHEREVER
YOU BUY BOOKS

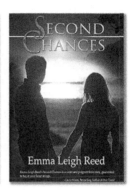

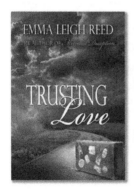

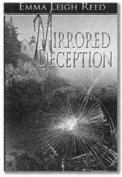

Made in the USA
Monee, IL
24 July 2021